Libby ~~was~~ **s** ~~ready~~ **n someone down below rang the doorbell.**

She groaned softly but didn't move. When it rang a second time she slipped a robe over her nightdress and went quickly downstairs. Before opening the door she peered into the porch, and with the moon's light filtering in saw the broad-shouldered outline of a man. Beside him was a small child dressed in pyjamas.

It all looked innocent enough, she decided. The two of them must be part of the family who'd moved in next door. Without any further delay she unlocked the door.

'Hello, Libby,' Nathan Gallagher said easily, as if it had only been yesterday that she'd last seen him.

She could feel her legs caving in at the shock of seeing him there...

Hello Again, Dear Reader

It's lovely to be back with you once more, having left golden beaches and Devon clotted cream teas for a while. In this new quartet of books we once again open the door to romance with all its tender magic as we share the lives of *The Doctors of Swallowbrook Farm*—a friendly surgery in a beautiful English country village, where Libby Hamilton and Nathan Gallagher pick up the pieces of something that should have happened long ago.

My son and daughter-in-law live close to a place like this, and every time I visit them the beauty of it enfolds me just as it does Libby and Nathan, in this first book of four. If you've enjoyed it do look out for Ruby and Hugo's story, coming next—another reminder that true love breaks down all barriers.

So, may I wish you happy reading as you turn the pages of these stories about *The Doctors of Swallowbrook Farm*.

Abigail Gordon

SWALLOWBROOK'S WINTER BRIDE

BY
ABIGAIL GORDON

MILLS & BOON

All the characters in this book have no existence outside the imagination
of the author, and have no relation whatsoever to anyone bearing the
same name or names. They are not even distantly inspired by any
individual known or unknown to the author, and all the incidents are
pure invention.

First published in Great Britain 2011
by Mills & Boon, an imprint of Harlequin (UK) Limited.
Harlequin (UK) Limited, Eton House,
18-24 Paradise Road, Richmond, Surrey TW9 1SR

© Abigail Gordon 2011

ISBN: 978 0 263 88614 6

Harlequin (UK) policy is to use papers that are natural, renewable
and recyclable products and made from wood grown in sustainable
forests. The logging and manufacturing process conform to the
legal environmental regulations of the country of origin.

Printed and bound in Spain
by Blackprint CPI, Barcelona

Abigail Gordon loves to write about the fascinating combination of medicine and romance from her home in a Cheshire village. She is active in local affairs, and is even called upon to write the script for the annual village pantomime! Her eldest son is a hospital manager, and helps with all her medical research. As part of a close-knit family, she treasures having two of her sons living close by, and the third one not too far away. This also gives her the added pleasure of being able to watch her delightful grandchildren growing up.

Recent titles by the same author:

FOR MY NEPHEW SHAUN MURRAY
AND HIS SON ANDREW
FAR AWAY FROM ME IN TEXAS

CHAPTER ONE

SPENDING two weeks in Spain with her best friend had been great, but as Libby Hamilton drove the last couple of miles to Swallowbrook village, nestling in a lakeland valley below the rugged beauty of the fells, she was happy to be back where she belonged.

A month ago, on what was not as frequent an occasion as she would like it to be, she had met up with Melissa Lombard for lunch in Manchester, and on seeing how pale and tired Libby looked, the only person she'd ever told what a mistake her tragically brief marriage had been had said, 'I'm going to our villa in Spain for a couple of weeks. That husband of mine can't go with me. There is a big audit due at the office and he's in charge. So why don't you join me, Libby? It would be lovely if you could.'

She'd hesitated and Melissa had said coaxingly, 'Surely they can manage without you at the Swallowbrook practice for once, and if they can't, they can get a temp. I'm no doctor but I think I can safely prescribe two weeks of lazing in the sun to bring some colour back to your cheeks.'

'It would be a change, I suppose,' Libby had agreed

wistfully. 'I haven't had any time off since Ian had the dreadful accident. It's as if I haven't been able to stop and think since the funeral. I guess I've been using work as an excuse these past few months.'

Melissa had nodded gravely and gone on to say sympathetically, 'So what better reason for joining me could there be than having spent months of hard graft without a break?'

Libby had smiled at her across the table and told her friend, 'You have just talked me into two weeks in Spain, Mel, but not a moment longer. Our senior partner, John Gallagher, retires at the end of the month and I've taken over as senior partner. He has virtually given up already, but I know if I ask him he'll take up the reins again for two more weeks while I have a break.'

Driving back now, alongside the fells beneath a harvest moon, she was feeling much more like her old self after a healthy dose of sun, sea and a complete rest. Yet as was always the case on the rare occasions she was absent from the practice, coming back to Swallowbrook and her cottage across the way from the surgery was heart-warming, and today was no exception.

The practice building had once been her childhood home. In those days it had been a farmhouse, but in her late teens it had been put up for sale due to her father's neglect of it after her mother had died, and it was now the village medical centre in the middle of the lakeside beauty spot.

When the lease had run out on the old practice premises and somewhere else had needed to be found, the spacious farm building had been an ideal choice. The outside of it was mostly unchanged, but the inside had been modernised and now provided health care for the hardy folk of Swallowbrook and the surrounding areas.

When the transfer had been made six years ago John Gallagher had been senior partner, with his son Nathan, also a doctor, working alongside him, and two years later Libby, who had gone straight into general practice after receiving her doctor's degree, had joined them as the third and youngest member of the trio.

But it had turned out that one of them had itchy feet, and where she had been content to stay in the place she loved best, Nathan Gallagher had other ideas in mind. He was three years older than her and she'd worshipped the dark-haired, dark-eyed, dynamic doctor since her early teens, but in those days she'd been just a kid with a brace on her teeth as far as he was concerned.

Though she'd never admit it to him, one of the reasons she'd joined the practice had been so that she could be near him, and another had been because the building had once been her home, and to be as close to it as she could she'd bought an empty farm cottage across the way.

When she'd joined the practice Nathan had seen that the girl who had always been hovering while they had been growing up had become a slender blonde with eyes like brown velvet and the warmest smile he'd ever seen. They'd shared a brief flirtation but he was aware that Libby had long since had a crush on him and didn't want to lead her on.

And besides he'd had his hands full with a fiancée who had been pushing hard for a gold band to go beside

the solitaire diamond on her finger and he had begun
to feel that the engagement had been a mistake because
he hadn't been as keen on the idea as she had been.

When he'd informed Libby that he was leaving the
practice to go and work abroad she'd been devastated.
'The engagement is off,' he'd told her, and it would
have been news she had been happy to hear if it hadn't
been followed by, 'So I'm free to work in Africa, which
is something I've always wanted to do. I've agreed to
take up a position in a hospital in a small town out there
where doctors are needed urgently.'

'How long will you be gone?' she'd asked with the
colour draining from her face.

'As long as it takes, I suppose, but my contract is for
three years.'

He'd noted the effect that the news of his departure
had had on her. 'Why don't you come along?' he'd suggested casually. 'There's always room for one more doctor out there.'

'No, thanks,' she'd replied hastily before she did
some crazy thing like letting her longing to be wherever
he was take over, and had gone on to say, 'It wouldn't
be fair to your father, two of us gone from the practice
at the same time, and *my* father is still around, don't
forget, forever sick and remorseful at having to sell
the farm. Also it has always been *my* dream to practise
medicine in the place that was once my home. I feel I
owe it to our community.'

She was almost home. As Libby took the next bend in
the road it was there, Swallowbrook, beautiful in the

moonlight, a familiar cluster of houses built out of lake-land stone, and outside The Mallard, the local pub, there was the usual gathering of fell walkers and locals seated on wooden benches, drinking the local brew.

Down a side turning not far away was Swallowbrook Medical Practice and across the way from it Lavender Cottage, where recently she'd spent far too many lonely nights at the end of long busy days.

The cottage was semi-detached. The property next to it had been on the market for quite some time and as she turned onto her drive she was surprised to see a van belonging to one of the big furniture stores in the nearby town pulling away from in front of it.

Her eyes widened. It was almost ten o'clock, de-liveries weren't usually made so late in the evening. It seemed from the number of lights blazing out into the night from the cottage next door that she was to be blessed, or otherwise, with new neighbours.

But she had other things to think about besides that, such as the longing to be back in her own bed after a quick cup of tea. The flight home hadn't taken long, but the airport procedures at the UK end had been slow and then there had been a thirty-miles-plus drive home after she'd collected her car from where it had been stored while she had been away, so now she was ready to flake out.

She hoped that the people who had moved into next door would be sociable and easy to get on with. Yet wasn't she the last person who should be concerned about socialising? She could barely remember what it was like to enjoy herself in the company of others.

After losing Ian in a fatal riding accident, a luke-warm marriage had come to an end, and since then the practice had been the only thing in her life that she could rely on for comfort and stability. As long as the new neighbours didn't intrude into that she supposed she would cope.

The surgery had been in darkness when she looked across, which was hardly surprising in the late evening, and as it was Friday would be closed all over the week-end. But as the head of the practice she would need to be there bright and early on Monday morning. Maybe during the weekend she would get the chance to meet the newcomers, but the main thing on her mind at the moment was sleep.

After the cup of tea that she'd been longing for on the last part of the journey home Libby climbed the stairs to her bedroom beneath the eaves and in moments was under the covers and ready to drift into oblivion when someone down below rang the doorbell.

She groaned softly but didn't move. When it rang a second time she slipped a robe over her nightdress and went quickly downstairs. Before opening the door she peered into the porch and with the moon's light filter-ing in saw the broad-shouldered outline of a man and beside him was a small child dressed in pyjamas.

It all looked innocent enough, she decided. The two of them must be part of the family who'd moved in next door, and without any further delay she unlocked the door.

'Hello, Libby,' Nathan Gallagher said easily, as if it had only been yesterday that she'd last seen her. 'We saw your car pull up a while ago and had no intention of disturbing you, but Toby needs his bedtime drink of milk, won't settle without it, and it's the one thing I've overlooked in the provisions I bought in the store this afternoon. I noticed you had a couple of pints that someone had delivered and wonder if you could spare one?'

She could feel her legs caving in at the shock of seeing him there.

'Come in,' she croaked, opening the door wide, and as they stepped inside she added, 'I'll get you one from the fridge.' With her glance on the tousle-haired small boy at his side she paused in the doorway of the kitchen. 'So it's you and your family who have moved into next door? You found yourself a wife while in Africa? It seems strange that your father never mentioned a thing!'

'Not exactly,' he said with a wry smile, and she wondered what that meant. Maybe the child's mother was a partner rather than a wife and she'd been rather quick to be asking those kinds of questions in any case.

Obviously Nathan hadn't come for a cosy chat about what he'd been doing during the last few years. Taking a pint of milk out of the fridge, she handed it to him and came up with a question of a more basic kind.

'Are your beds made up? Tell your little boy's mother I can lend you some bedding if you haven't had time to get them sorted.'

'Thanks, but everything is fine,' was the reply. 'We've been here since early this morning. As soon as Toby has had his milk he will be settling down for sleep in a small single bed next to mine. It's been a long day so I don't think either of us will need much rocking.'

'How long have you been back in the UK?' she asked as he was about to depart with the little boy clutching his hand tightly.

'A month. We've been in London until now on business, but I was anxious to get away from the crowds. I want Toby to grow up in Swallowbrook like we did, and the vacant cottage next door to yours seemed to be the perfect answer.'

Answer to what? she wondered. Whatever it was it wouldn't be anything to do with her. He'd asked her to go out to Africa with him all that time ago because they were short of doctors, not because he'd wanted her near, and at the time she'd come up with a few reasons for refusing.

It was like a knife in her heart seeing him with his small son. It meant that he'd found someone that he *did* want, while she'd been letting common sense fly out of the window by agreeing to marry Ian, whose interests had revolved around his horses and pleasure, and seen her career as a hindrance to his lifestyle, instead of giving it meaning.

With no wish to remind herself of how all that had ended she switched her thoughts to the mother of the child and wondered where she was. She probably had other things to do, having just moved into next door, and curious though she might be, there was no way she was going to ask Nathan why the sleeping arrangements he'd described didn't sound as if Toby's mother was included in them.

When Libby went back upstairs to bed the feeling of tiredness had been replaced by bleak amazement as she recalled those incredible moments with Nathan and the silent child. Wide-eyed and disbelieving, her gaze was fixed on the dividing wall between the two properties.

He would be sleeping at the other side of it, she thought. Just a short time ago she'd seen him in the flesh, heard him speak, watched him smile a strange smile when she'd asked him if he had married while out in Africa.

He'd said, 'Not exactly,' and she cringed at her unseemly haste in asking the question only seconds after he'd appeared at her door. It would have been the last thing she would have come up with if he hadn't had the boy with him.

Had his father known for the last month that he was back in England and not told her? If that *was* the case, it would have been on Nathan's instructions. John would never do anything like that to her.

Tomorrow she would have to prepare herself for meeting the little boy's mother with pleasantness and a warm welcome to Swallowbrook, while hoping that she would be able to hide her true feelings, and with those kinds of thoughts to cope with she got up and put the kettle on for a second time.

Behind the dividing wall Nathan was not asleep but Toby was, curled up and content after having drunk some of the milk that Libby had provided. As the man looked down at the child the stresses and strains, the sorrow and confusion of past months seemed less dreadful because he was back home in Swallowbrook once more.

The last time he'd seen Libby Hamilton had also been from the shelter of a porch, but not the one next door. It had been in the shadowed stone porch of the village church after he'd flung himself out of the taxi that had brought him from the airport, hoping that he might get the chance to speak to her before she became the wife of Ian Jefferson.

He'd needed to know if it was because of his leaving that she was marrying the pleasure-loving owner of the local stables…on the rebound. Or if the feelings that she'd said she had for himself had been just a passing attraction that she'd soon moved on from and there was no longer any need for him to carry the burden of guilt that his leaving her had created.

A delayed flight had denied him the chance to clear the air between them and he'd arrived at the church just as the vicar had pronounced them man and wife. As he'd watched Libby smile up at her new husband he'd turned and departed as quickly as he'd come, deciding in that moment he had his answer. Her feelings for him *had* been a passing fancy and a prize fool he would have appeared if anyone had seen him hovering in the church porch for a glimpse of her.

When he'd reached the lych gate in the churchyard a bus had pulled up beside him on the pavement and he'd boarded it, uncaring where it was bound in his haste to get away before he was seen.

As he'd waited for a flight to take him back to where he'd come from he'd thought sombrely that his arrogance all that time ago when in her despair at the thought of him going away Libby had confessed her love for him and been told he wasn't interested, had only been exceeded by him expecting her to want to talk to him of all people on her wedding day.

She had turned up at the airport on the morning he had left for Africa and been the only one there. He'd said his farewells to his father the night before and told everyone else he didn't want any send-offs, so it had been a surprise, and he'd had to admit a pleasant one, to see her there.

They had been due to call his flight any time and during those last few moments in the UK Libby had begged him not to go. 'I love you, Nathan,' she'd pleaded. 'I always have. Until I awoke this morning I had accepted that you were going out of my life. Then suddenly I knew I had to see you just one more time.

'I know the importance of the work you are going to do in Africa, but there would still be time for that when we'd had *our* time, some life together in happiness and contentment and maybe brought up a family.'

She had chosen the most inopportune moment to make her plea, with only minutes to spare before he boarded the plane, *and* with the memory tugging at him of a failed engagement not so long ago that had done neither he nor his fiancée any credit.

There had been tears in her eyes but instead of making him want to comfort her he'd reacted in the opposite way and been brusque and offhand as he'd told her, 'How can you face me with something like this at such a time, Libby? I'm due to leave in a matter of minutes.

Just forget me. Don't wait around. Relationships aren't on my agenda at present.'

Then, ashamed of his churlishness, he'd bent to give her a peck on the cheek. Instead their lips had met and within seconds it had all changed.

He'd been kissing her as if he'd just walked into light out of darkness and it would have gone on for ever if a voice hadn't been announcing that his flight was ready for boarding.

As common sense had returned he'd said it again. 'Don't wait around for me, Libby.' And almost before he'd finished speaking she'd been rushing towards the exit as if she couldn't get away from him fast enough.

Aware that his behaviour had left a lot to be desired, and cursing himself for trampling on what was left of her schoolgirl crush, he'd vowed that he would phone her when he arrived at his destination and apologise for his flippancy, but in the chaos he'd found when he'd got there his private life had become non-existent, until he'd received his father's phone call some months later to say Libby was getting married on the coming Saturday.

Then it had all come flooding back—her tears, the loveliness of her, and his own arrogance in brushing to one side her feelings for him by telling her not to wait for him, indicating in the most presumptuous way that *he* wasn't interested in *her*.

But, of course, by then it had been too late. How could he ever forget how happy she had looked when the vicar had made his pronouncement to say Libby and Ian were man and wife? And he'd thought how wrong he'd been in considering that she might be marrying Jefferson on the rebound.

Now, as he looked down at Toby, young and defence-less beneath the covers, he knew that there would be barriers to break down in coming months and bridges to build, not just in one part of his life but in the whole structure of it, because his contract in Africa was up. He was home for good, and coming back to Swallowbrook was his first step towards normality.

He'd done nothing when he'd heard that Jefferson had died. To have appeared on the scene then might have seemed like he'd been waiting in the wings and it would not have been the case. But now he'd had no choice but to come back to England because his best friend and his wife had been amongst tourists drowned on a sinking ferry somewhere abroad. The tragedy had changed his life and that of the sleeping child for ever.

As she sat hunched over the teapot Libby was thinking what a mess her life had turned into in the three years since she'd last laid eyes on Nathan. Anxious to prove to the world, but most importantly to herself, that her feelings for him were dead and buried she'd turned to Ian Jefferson, someone who had already asked her to marry him twice and been politely refused.

And so six months later, with Nathan's never-to-be-forgotten comments at the airport still painfully re-membered, she'd agreed to marry Ian at his third time of asking.

They'd been reasonably happy at first, living in Lavender Cottage, across from the surgery, but as the months had gone by she had discovered that Ian had merely wanted a wife, any wife, to give him standing in the village, and the blonde doctor from the practice had been his first choice.

Marriage hadn't made him any less keen on spending endless hours on the golf course, sailing on the lake by Swallowbrook and, while his staff looked after the stables, riding around the countryside on various of his horses, which had left him with little time to comprehend the burden of care that Libby carried with her position at the practice, a position that left her with little time or energy to share in his constant round of pleasure.

It had been one night whilst out riding that he had been thrown from a frisky mare and suffered serious injuries that had proved fatal, leaving her to face another gap in her life that was sad and traumatic, but not as heartbreaking as being separated from Nathan.

When she'd drunk the teapot dry Libby went to bed for the second time and after tossing and turning for most of the night drifted into sleep as dawn was breaking over the fells. She was brought into wakefulness a short time later by voices down below at the bottom of the drive and when she went to the window the dairy farmer who delivered her milk was chatting to Nathan, who, judging from the amount of milk he was buying off him, was making sure that he and Toby would not have to go begging for his bedtime drink again.

Not wanting to be seen watching him, she went slowly back to bed, grateful that it was Saturday with no need to get up if she didn't want to, and as a pale sun filtered into her bedroom she began to go over the astonishing events of the previous night.

Nathan is back in Swallowbrook, a voice in her mind was saying, *but not because of you. He has a family. He has made his choice and it has to be better than the one you made.*

She surfaced at lunchtime in a calmer state of mind and, dressed in slacks and a smart sweater, went to the village for food and various other things she needed from the shops after being away.

There had been no sign of anyone from next door when she'd set off, but Nathan's car had still been in front of the cottage, so either they were inside out of sight or had ventured out for the boy to see where they had come to live, and the man to reacquaint himself with the place where he had been brought up amongst people who had been his patients and friends.

To make her way home she had to pass the park next to the school that strangely for a Saturday was empty, except for Nathan and the boy, who was moving from one amusement to another in the children's play area.

Don't stop, she told herself. *Nathan has had all morning to see you again if he wanted to, so don't give him the satisfaction of thinking you've followed him here.*

The two of them looked lonely and lost in the deserted park. He was pushing Toby on one of the swings, but on seeing her passing lifted him off. Now they were coming towards her and she was getting a better look at the prodigal doctor than in her mesmerised state the night before.

His time in Africa had taken its toll of him, she observed as he drew nearer. He was leaner, giving off less of the dynamism that had so attracted her to him over the years, but his hair was the same, the dark thatch of it curling above his ears, and his eyes were still the unreadable dark hazel that they'd always been where she was concerned.

'I can't believe you were going to go past without speaking,' he said as they drew level.

'Why?' she asked steadily. 'What is there to say?'

'On my part that I was sorry to hear of Jefferson's fatal accident, and for another—'

He was interrupted by the child at his side tugging at his hand and saying, 'Can I go on the slide, Uncle Nathan?'

'Yes, go along,' he replied. 'I'll be with you in a moment.' As Libby observed him in a daze of noncomprehension he explained, 'I'm in the process of adopting Toby. Both his parents are dead. They were lost when a ferry sank while they were touring Europe. Thankfully he was saved. His father was my best friend and I am the boy's godfather.

'I went out to bring him home when it happened and applied to adopt him as there were no other relatives to lay claim to him. The paperwork is going through at the moment and soon he will be legally mine.'

'How do you cope?' she asked as the heartache of thinking that Nathan had a family of his own began to recede.

'It was difficult in the beginning because although Toby knew me well enough, naturally it was his mummy and daddy he wanted. He is adjusting slowly to the situation, yet is loath to ever let me out of his sight.'

Poor little one, she thought, poor godfather...*poor me. How am I going to cope having Nathan living next door to me with the memory of what he said that day at the airport still crystal clear? He has never been back to Swallowbrook since and now, as if he hadn't hurt me enough then, he has chosen to live in the cottage next to mine.*

He was observing her questioningly in the silence that her thoughts had created, and keen to escape the scrutiny of his stare she asked, 'How old is Toby?'

'He's just five, and the ferry catastrophe occurred three months ago. You might have read about it in the press or seen an account of it on television.'

That was unlikely, she thought wryly. In the mornings it was a quick breakfast, then across the way to the practice, and in the evenings the day's events had to be assimilated and paperwork brought up to date.

'What will you do now that you're here?' she asked, trying to sound normal. 'Enrol Toby at the village school?'

'I've already done so and am not sure how he is going to react to yet another change in his life. I have to tread softly with his young mind. He soon gets upset, which is to be expected, of course.'

She felt tears prick. It was all so sad that Nathan had been forced to take on such a responsibility *and* felt he had to return to Swallowbrook for the child's sake if nothing else.

As they went to wait for Toby at the bottom of a

small slide the man by her side was smiling, which was strange, as given what he had just told her he hadn't got a lot to smile about.

CHAPTER TWO

It was a lot to take in. Only yesterday she had been flying home from two refreshing weeks in Spain with Melissa. Today she was in the park with Nathan and a child that he was adopting, and though she felt great sympathy for their loss she couldn't help but feel relieved that Nathan hadn't found himself a ready-made wife and family during his time in Africa.

If she had known he was coming back to Swallowbrook in the near future she would have had time to prepare herself for meeting up again with the man who had made it so painfully clear on parting that he didn't return her feelings. But instead it was as if she'd been thrown in at the deep end.

She was bending to pick up the bag with her food shopping inside when he forestalled her by saying easily, 'I'll take that,' and to Toby, who was coming down the slide for the umpteenth time, 'Time to go, Tobias.'

When the little one had joined them they walked back to their respective properties in silence. As they were about to separate Libby asked, 'Have you been to see your father?'

He nodded. 'Yes, we went to see him yesterday in a gap between deliveries of furniture and other household goods, and before you came back from wherever you'd been.'

'I'd been to Spain for a fortnight with a friend for a much-needed break,' she said coolly, 'and hope to be on top form at the practice on Monday.'

'Ah, yes,' he said vaguely, as if he had only a faint recollection of the place. 'Dad told me he plans to hand the practice over to you.'

'Yes. I'm delighted to have his trust. I think I love that place almost as much as he does. I couldn't bear to see it close down with his retirement and said as much to him.'

'So you'll be a doctor short now that Dad's gone,' he commented as she fumbled around in her handbag for the door keys.

'Yes. John and I have seen one or two hopefuls, but he was strangely reluctant to make a decision and now I see why. He's been waiting for you to come home.'

He nodded. 'Possibly, but Dad has only just found out about Toby and now realises that it wouldn't work. I need to be there to see him into school in the morning and to be waiting when he comes out in the afternoon.'

'Part time?'

'Yes, unless I was to employ a nanny, but he has had enough changes to put up with already without my putting him in the charge of a stranger.'

She had the keys in her hand now, but before putting them in the lock had one thing to say that hopefully would end this strange moment.

'Your father might want you back in the practice, Nathan, but I'm not sure that I do. I have my life planned and it doesn't include working with *you*. At the moment the doctors in the practice are myself and Hugo Lawrence, who came to us from general practice in Bournemouth to be where he could give support to his sister and her children. She was widowed some time ago and isn't coping very well.

'There are three nurses, three part-time receptionists and Gordon Jessup is still practice manager from when you were there before, and with a district nurse and a midwife attached to the surgery we have an excellent team with just one more doctor needed to make it complete. I'm not enjoying the interview process much—it's not really my area of expertise. Also it's proving difficult to fill the vacancy. We face stiff competition from urban practices, lots of younger doctors seem put off by the remoteness of the community, but we don't want anyone too near retirement either. The patients and the practice need stability. I've already heard a few rumblings from those concerned about your father's departure.'

'But you don't want me?'

'No, not particularly, but as the senior partner I suppose I should forget personal feelings and consider the best interests of the patients. They would most likely be thrilled to see the Gallagher name remain above the threshold. And I suppose you working part time might work very well for us—it wasn't something I'd considered before.' In a voice that sounded as if she was reciting her own epitaph she went on, 'So, yes, if that is what you want, come and join us.'

'Thanks a bunch,' he said with a quizzical smile, knowing she felt he deserved her lack of enthusiasm. Though would Libby still feel the same if she knew about his last-minute attempt to speak to her before her wedding? But no way was he going to use that to turn her round to his way of thinking.

Apart from the practice, which she would serve well as head, there must be little for her to rejoice about in any other sphere of her life now that Jefferson was gone.

He hadn't been expecting a fanfare of trumpets on his return to Swallowbrook, or Libby throwing herself into his arms, but he had been hoping she might have forgiven him for what he'd said in those moments of parting long ago.

It had been partly for Toby's sake that he'd come back to Swallowbrook, but always there had been the hope that one day he and Libby might meet again and a chance to make up for the past would present itself.

'Do you want to come to the practice on Monday morning to discuss your hours? I could make sure I'm free at ten o'clock,' she was suggesting.

'Yes, please.'

He'd said it meekly but the glint in the dark eyes looking into hers said differently.

He hasn't changed, she thought. Nathan Gallagher is still a law unto himself. She put her key in the lock and told him, 'So ten o'clock on Monday it is.'

Bending, she planted a swift kiss on Toby's smooth

cheek and said in gentle contrast to the businesslike tone she'd used to Nathan, 'We have a lovely school here, Toby, I'm sure you'll like it.'

He was a wiry child with a mop of fair curls, and so far hadn't said a word to her, but that was about to change.

'Are you my uncle's friend?' he asked.

Aware of Nathan's gaze on her, she said carefully, 'No, I am just someone he used to work with.'

Having satisfied himself on that, Toby had another question that was more personal.

'Have *you* got any children?'

'No, I'm afraid not.'

'Why?'

'Because I have never found anyone nice enough to be their daddy,' she told him.

'So why—?' The small questioner hadn't finished, but didn't get the chance to continue the interrogation as Nathan was taking his hand and preparing to depart.

'Say goodbye to Dr Hamilton,' he said, and with half a smile for her, 'Until Monday, then, at ten o'clock, Libby.'

She nodded, and with sanctuary beckoning opened the door and went inside.

It seemed as if Sunday was going to be a non-event day and Libby was thankful for it. While she was having breakfast she saw Nathan and Toby go down the drive and get into the car with fishing rods and surmised they were going to spend some time with his father at the pine lodge he'd recently moved into.

When they'd gone she did what she'd been doing ever since their discussion about Nathan coming back into the practice, which was wishing she hadn't been so overbearing in her manner.

She'd made it clear without actually putting it into words that she hadn't forgotten that day at the airport, and wasn't going to fall into the same trap ever again where he was concerned. Yet if that *was* the case, why had she been so happy to discover that he wasn't married with a family?

What he was doing for Toby was so special it brought tears to her eyes every time she thought about it. Through no fault of his own Nathan had taken on the role of single father with the burden of care that went with it, and all *she* had done so far was cut him down to size about working in the practice, which was where he belonged now that the African contract was finished.

He'd said he was sorry to hear about what had happened to Ian and she'd thought that he didn't know that disillusion had followed swiftly after a marriage that had been a mistake from the start. Remembering Toby's curiosity of the day before, the answer she'd come up with for not having children had been true. She wouldn't have wanted a child from a union as empty as hers and Ian's had been.

With the afternoon and evening looming ahead, she decided to resort to one of her favourite pastimes, a sail on one of the steamers that ploughed through the waters of the lake countless times each day, and on disembarking at the other end would have her evening meal at her favourite restaurant beside the moorings.

The boat was full and she stood holding onto the rail, taking in the splendour of the new hospital on the lake-side as they sailed past and gazing enviously at houses built from the pale grey stone of the area with their own private landing stages and fishing rights.

She could see farms in the distance, surrounded by green meadows where livestock grazed, and high up above, towering on the skyline, as familiar as her own face, were the fells, the rugged guardians of the lakes.

Had Nathan the same love of this lakeland valley as she had? she wondered. Had he ever longed to be back in the place where his roots were during those hot days in Africa? If he had it would be at least one thing they had in common, she thought wryly, and wondered how many fish he and Toby had caught in the river beside John's pine lodge.

The answers to the questions in her mind were nearer than she thought as his voice came from behind and as she turned swiftly he said, 'I used to dream I was doing the round trip on one of these boats when I was far away. Sometimes it was the only thing that kept me sane.'

Before he could elaborate further Toby was tugging at her sleeve and announcing excitedly, 'We've caught some fish, Dr Hamilton.'

'Really!' she exclaimed, suitably impressed. 'How many?'

'Two. A salmon and a pike,' he announced.

'But we had to throw the pike back into the water because it is a special fish,' Nathan explained.

'And so where is the salmon now?'

'Dad is cooking it for us for when we get back,' Nathan informed her, 'but first I wanted Toby to sail on the steamer.' In a low voice he added, 'I'm sorry if you feel that I'm everywhere you turn, Libby. I had no idea you were on board. Would you like to come back and join us? There will be plenty of fish to spare.'

Temptation was staring her in the face, but she was not going to succumb. It was going to be a strictly working relationship that she had in mind for them and nothing else, so she said politely, 'Thanks for the invitation, but I have a regular table booked at my favourite restaurant and wouldn't want to let them down.'

He was getting the message, Nathan thought. Not exactly the cold shoulder, but the 'I have not forgotten' treatment, and he wished, as he had done many times before, that he had got in touch with Libby the moment he'd arrived in Africa and at the very least apologised to the beautiful girl whose heart he had broken.

But the timing had been wrong all along the line, beginning with him discovering at the airport that he wasn't as indifferent to Libby Hamilton as he'd thought he was, followed by the knowledge that his flight was due to be called any moment, and overriding everything else, at the forefront of his mind, had been his commitment to the hospital in Africa.

The outcome of it had been that he'd been dumbstruck by the suddenness of it all, and had sent her away, then months later there had been his dash across half the world to speak to Libby before she became Jefferson's wife but he'd missed his chance by seconds and returned to Africa with his questions unanswered.

But now *he* was home, back in Swallowbrook once more, and s*he* was minus a husband, though undoubtedly still reeling from grief, and he was still no nearer to knowing how deep her feelings had been that day at the airport. It could have been a carry-over from her schoolgirl crush. In fact, it must have been a short-lived infatuation judging from the speed with which she'd married Ian Jefferson, and there had certainly been no chemistry between them since he'd turned up out of the blue with Toby. Plenty of being put in his place but no rousing of the senses for either of them as far as he could tell.

'Fine,' he said easily in answer to her refusal.

She'd looked so solitary standing by the rail, watching the steamer cutting its way through the water on its journey across the lake, that he hadn't been able to resist inviting her to join them at his father's place but again the barriers had been up.

When they arrived at the moorings at the far side Nathan and Toby stayed on the steamer in readiness for sailing back and Libby, after a brief goodbye, went to dine at the restaurant that she'd used as an excuse to refuse his invitation.

The fact that she'd already been on her way there didn't make her excuse to Nathan any less untruthful. Although she dined there frequently she didn't have a table booked on a regular basis, and for once she didn't enjoy the food that was put in front of her.

She caught the last steamer back before the light went and then made her way to Swallowbrook in a sombre mood with the thought of starting work as senior partner with Nathan as her newest employee the following morning.

A knock on the door of her consulting room at precisely ten o'clock announced Nathan's arrival and Libby pushed back her chair and went to let him in.

He was alone and the first thing she said was, 'Where's Toby?'

'He's playing with the children's toys in the waiting room. One of the receptionists is keeping an eye on him,' was the reply.

Seating himself across from her, he asked, 'Did you enjoy your meal?'

'No, not really,' she admitted.

'Why was that?'

'I don't know. Maybe it was because I like freshly caught salmon.'

'But not the guy who reeled it in?'

'I have no feelings either way about *him*,' she said and followed it with, 'I do have patients waiting, Nathan, so shall we proceed? What hours would you be available to join us here?'

'Half past nine to three-thirty when the primary children finish,' he said promptly. 'We've been to see the headmaster before coming here and it's sorted for Toby to start tomorrow. Today I'm going to take him into town for his uniform and a satchell.

'If it's all right with you, I feel that Wednesday would

be a good day for me to settle back into the practice. It will leave me with tomorrow free in case Toby is reluctant to go when the moment arrives. He's had so many changes in his life over recent months I wouldn't be surprised.'

'Wednesday will be fine,' she assured him, and had to admire the way he had his priorities sorted. Getting back to the reason for his presence on the premises, she informed him, 'Your father's consulting room at the opposite end of the corridor is vacant, and as all the staff are new since you were last with us, apart from Gordon, the practice manager, I'll introduce you to them while you are here if you like.'

'Yes, sure,' he said easily. 'It would seem that the only things familiar to me are going to be the layout of the place...and you, Libby.'

In your dreams, she thought. She would accept him as a neighbour because she had no choice, and as a colleague because she knew his worth as a doctor, but that was the limit of it. Familiar she was not going to be.

Nathan didn't stay long after the introductions had been made. He separated Toby from the assortment of toys provided to keep small patients happy and took him for his school uniform of dark green and gold, leaving Libby to ponder on how much, or how little, she was going to enjoy working with him again.

She saw the two of them go past the surgery window the following morning and a lump came up in her throat to see the small boy resplendent in a green and gold blazer and matching T-shirt and shorts with Nathan holding his hand and looking down at him protectively.

She'd once dreamed of a similar scenario for the two of them, loving each other, loving the children they created, but that was all it had been, a dream. In utter foolishness she'd turned to someone else and that had been a *nightmare*, so where did she go from here? she wondered.

Yet she knew the answer to the question almost before she'd asked it of herself. She and Nathan were going nowhere. That way she would steer clear of any more heartbreak connected with the men in her life. She'd shown herself to be a poor judge when it came to that.

She'd thought sometimes during the long years he'd been gone, Why shouldn't he have said what he did? At least he hadn't strung her along into thinking he was interested in her when he wasn't, which was what Ian had done, pursued the attractive young doctor at the practice when she was at her most vulnerable to satisfy his ego.

But there was work to do, patients to see, and she needed normality to keep her mind free from the events of a very strange weekend.

As she rose from her desk, intending to make a quick coffee before the next patient appeared, Nathan was passing again, homeward bound this time. When she waved he smiled, gave the thumbs-up sign and went on his way, leaving her with the feeling of unreality that had been there ever since she'd opened her door to him on Friday night.

* * *

Henrietta Weekes was a regular visitor at the practice with most of her problems associated with a failing heart due to having had scarlet fever when she was a child. A smart, intelligent woman, she usually coped with them calmly with little fuss, but today she was in distress and needing to see a doctor.

After checking her heart, Libby exclaimed, 'How on earth have you managed to get here in this state, Henrietta?'

'My son has brought me,' she gasped.

'I'm glad to hear you haven't walked,' she told her soberly. 'Your heart is completely out of control and is affecting your lungs. I'm sending you to the coronary unit at the new hospital straight away by ambulance. You will be attended to more quickly that way than if your son was to take you. I'll get one of the nurses to help you back into the waiting room to join him while I send out an emergency call. You're an amazing woman, Henrietta, I'm not giving up on you. Once they get you into Coronary Care, you'll be in safe hands.'

'If I live that long,' she said with a grimace of a smile, and Libby thought it was typical of the woman that she was facing up to what might happen with the same sort of stoicism that was always there in every crisis that brought her to the surgery for help. Her family, who were devoted to her, must live on a knife edge where their mother's health was concerned.

As the day progressed like any other busy Monday at the practice there was no time to wonder how Nathan was occupying himself until Toby came out of school, or let her thoughts wander to how a small orphaned boy might be coping on his first day. Maybe she would find out tonight when her day at the practice was over and she was back at the cottage.

She was about to make a snack meal for herself that evening when there was a knock on the door, and when she opened it Toby was smiling up at her and announcing, 'Uncle Nathan says would you like to come and eat with us?'

Clever uncle, she thought. *He knows I won't refuse if he sends Toby with the invitation, but didn't he get the message when we were on the steamer and I came up with an excuse for not accepting the invitation to join them at his father's place?*

He was gazing up at her innocently, waiting for an answer, so she said, 'Yes, that would be lovely, Toby. When shall I come?'

Taking her hand in his, he tugged her towards him and said, 'Now, Dr Hamilton.' And having just been given her full title once again, she thought that if she and Toby were going to seeing much of each other he must be allowed to call her something simpler than that.

'We're having fish fingers and ice cream, Toby's choice,' Nathan told her when she appeared hesitantly in the kitchen doorway, 'to celebrate his first day at school,' adding in a low voice that was for her ears only, 'which he has enjoyed, thank goodness.'

'I can imagine how relieved you are about that,' she replied with her glance on the boy who had gone into the garden and was kicking a ball around while he waited to be fed.

He nodded sombrely but didn't reply. Instead he asked, 'How do you like my efforts to make it seem like a home to him?'

She looked around her. 'Impressive. Just the right blend of luxury and cosiness.'

'That is what I wanted to achieve. There wasn't much of that about where I was based in Africa, and since I've become involved in adopting Toby we've been living in a rented apartment in London while I've been sorting out his parents' affairs for him.

'Now that we've crossed the hurdle of his first day at school and are settling into this place I'm hoping that we can put down some roots and become part of the community, the same as I was before.'

'You can't be a much bigger part of the community than serving them as a GP,' she pointed out, 'or have you changed your mind about tomorrow?'

'No, of course not. *I'm* looking forward to it even if *you* aren't.'

He watched the colour rise in her cheeks and thought that where she'd been beautiful before, now she was divine. Still, she'd made it quite clear that their relationship was to be purely professional and he supposed he deserved no more after the way they had parted.

But only he knew the truth of the affair that had ended in him going to work abroad. He still shuddered at the thought of it, and the fact that Libby had been dragged into its aftermath that day at the airport would always be on his conscience.

His broken engagement to Felice Stopford all that time ago had made him wary of romantic love. It was an emotion he'd felt he hadn't fully understood, and it had come through in the way he'd been so dismissive when Libby had told him how much she cared for him.

To Felice 'love' had meant money and position, expensive gifts, wining and dining, holidays abroad in plush hotels, and he had begun to realise that she was not for him about the same time that Libby had joined the practice.

He'd met his fiancée at a charity luncheon where he had been asked to speak about health care in the area and she'd stood out amongst the soberly dressed audience like a beacon on a hilltop. Dark-haired, voluptuous and quite charming, she'd made a beeline for him when it had finished and introduced herself as an American fundraiser representing similar organisations back in the States.

Her invitation to lunch had been the beginning of a romance that had started on a high and finished on the lowest of lows because he'd gradually discovered that her values were not the same as his. He'd found her to be greedy and shallow as he'd got to know her better and been uneasy about her eagerness for them to marry.

When he'd called the engagement off she'd gone storming back to the States and shortly afterwards he'd discovered through a colleague of hers that she'd had a doting elderly husband back there that she'd been eager to unload to make way for someone like himself.

That item of news had sickened him, made him feel tarnished, and pointed him in the direction of working

overseas, which was something he'd been considering
before he'd got to know Felice and been sidetracked. It
was into that state of affairs that Libby had opened her
heart to him. Felice had made him suspicious of love
and ultimately it was Libby who'd suffered. The least
he could do for her now was to abide by her terms and
respect her wishes where their relationship was concerned.

By the time they'd finished eating Toby's eyelids were
drooping and Nathan said, 'It's been a long day for him,
Libby. If you'll excuse us, I'll get him tucked up for the
night. There are magazines or the TV if you want to
wait until I come down.' And picking the sleepy child
up in his arms, he carried him upstairs.

When they'd gone she went into the kitchen. He'd
mentioned magazines and television but there was the
tidying up after the meal that would be waiting for him
when he came back downstairs. If there was one thing
she could do for him it was that, then she would go as
quickly as she had come while her resolve to be distant
with him was still there.

The kitchen was immaculate and she was seated at the
table, scribbling a note to say thanks for the meal, when
he came down. As she swung round to face him he was
observing her with raised brows.

'I was about to go and was leaving you a note,' she
explained.

'Making your getaway while I wasn't around?' he
questioned dryly.

'Yes, something like that,' she told him with cool defiance.

He sighed. 'Go ahead, then, Libby, don't let me stop you. I can see it's going to be a bundle of laughs at the surgery tomorrow.'

'Not necessarily,' she told him levelly, 'as long as we both behave like adults.'

His jaw was set tightly. 'Why don't you come right out with it and tell me that I'm not forgiven for what I said at the airport that day?' *And have regretted ever since.*

This was laying it on the line with a vengeance, she thought, but was in no mood to bring her innermost feelings out into the open. She'd had a disastrous marriage since then and was older and wiser in many ways.

'What you said long ago is in the past. I never give it a thought. We've both moved on after all,' she said flatly. With a sudden weakening of her resolve, she added, 'So why don't we just get on with living next door to each other, working side by side at the practice, and leave it at that?'

The line of his jaw was still tight, the glint still in his eyes, but his voice was easy enough as he said, 'Fine by me. I'll see you tomorrow, Libby.' As she got to her feet he said, 'Thanks for tidying the kitchen. I'll do the same for you one day if I'm ever invited across your threshold.'

Having no intention of taking him up on that comment, she gave a half-smile and, reaching out for the door handle, said, 'I hope that Toby is as happy at school tomorrow as he's been today.' She stepped out into the gathering dark. 'Goodnight, Nathan.'

'Goodnight to you too,' he said as he stood in the open doorway and watched her walk quickly down his drive and up her own.

When he heard her door click to behind her he went back inside and wondered if him joining the practice would cause less tension or more between the two of them.

CHAPTER THREE

LIBBY tried not to keep looking at her watch the next morning as she waited for Nathan to arrive to start his first shift. In spite of her personal feelings she knew he would be as good as his word. The same as his devotion to Toby would not falter. With Nathan's loving support he seemed to be settling well into his new life. Sadly the one thing he would need the most at his tender age was a loving mother and what his adopted father intended doing about that she didn't know.

But aware that the man in question still possessed the attractions that had drawn *her* to him, she imagined that there would soon be members of her sex queuing to play the mother role.

Not that she was going to throw herself into the running, of course. She'd tried to make it clear once more last night that there could be nothing more between them, but he was the one who had raked up the past and caused her to put on an act regarding something she would never forget, and no way did she want it to happen again.

She was going to be pleasant but aloof from now on—no more harking back to times past, if only because of the humiliation that came with the memory of them. Life had treated her badly so far with two unpleasant experiences that most women would never have to face in a lifetime, and since Ian's death she was resolved never to let herself be hurt again in that way.

Besides, now wasn't the time to be thinking about Nathan—she had patients to see, starting with octogenarian Donald Johnson and when he appeared she asked, 'What can I do for you today, Mr Johnson? Are you here about the tests I sent you for?'

'Aye, I am,' was the reply.

'Yes, I thought so,' she said, and told him, 'I received a letter from the hospital this morning regarding the tests on your kidneys that I requested and was going to phone you. It would seem that one of them isn't functioning and the other, although performing quite well, is not at full strength.'

'I see. So one of my kidneys has had it and the other is limping along,' he commented grumpily.

She smiled across at him. 'It isn't such a gloomy outlook as it seems. Our kidneys do gradually deteriorate as we get older, but lots of people survive with only one. We hear of those who have given a healthy kidney to someone else to avoid renal failure and still live a good life with just the one, and although in your case the one that is still working is past its best, I feel sure that it will continue to do its job.

'The hospital say that they will want to see you every three months, which means they are going to keep a close watch on them, so for the present I would put your worries to one side.'

'I wouldn't have had any worries if you hadn't sent me for those tests,' he protested.

'It's standard procedure for a GP to arrange for those sorts of procedures for the elderly,' she explained. 'It won't have made your kidneys any worse, and now you will have regular checks, which can't be bad, surely?'

'Aye, I suppose you're right,' he agreed reluctantly, getting to his feet. 'I'm going fishing at John Gallagher's place this afternoon, that'll cheer me up a bit, and John let slip that Nathan is back in the village and he has a young'un to care for too. Is he going to be doctoring in this place again?'

'Yes, he starts later on this morning, once he's dropped his son off at school.'

'That *is* good news!' he exclaimed. 'It will be like old times.'

Not exactly, she thought as he went to make way for the next patient on her list.

'It was a stroke of genius, bringing Nathan Gallagher back into the practice,' Hugo Lawrence said when he appeared in the doorway of her consulting room in the middle of the morning. 'Being out of touch with the NHS for so long doesn't seem to have affected his performance. He's on top of the job from the word go by the looks of it.'

She smiled at his enthusiasm, but couldn't help pointing out that it had been more a case of Nathan taking it for granted he would be slotting back into the practice. There had been no inspired thinking on her part with regard to his arrival at dead on half past nine in a smart suit, shirt and tie and oozing cool competence.

The fact that underneath it he was wary of making the wrong move where she was concerned would have amazed her if she had been aware of it. As it was, his presence was a cause for pain and pleasure in equal parts and she would be relieved when the first day of his return to the practice was over.

When she'd asked about Toby starting his second day at school he had said there'd been just a moment's reluctance to go into lines in the schoolyard, as was the custom before the children went to their classes. But he'd seemed happy enough as he was trooping in with the rest of them.

She'd sensed anxiety in him at that moment, although seconds later he'd been seeing his first patient as if he'd never been away from the place and she'd told herself to stop involving herself in his affairs or she would be asking for more heartache than she had already.

'Do you want to do the home visits to reacquaint yourself with the area?' she enquired when the three doctors stopped for their lunch break. 'Or would you rather give it a few days to settle in before you do that?'

He hesitated. 'Maybe tomorrow, if you don't mind. I would rather be around if the school should need to get in touch after the little episode this morning. I know it sounds as if I'm fussing, but...'

Caring wasn't fussing, she wanted to tell him as a lump came up in her throat, but hadn't she just been telling herself to stay aloof from his affairs? So instead she replied coolly, 'Yes, of course. I'll do them, and leave Hugo and yourself to see the rest of the patients on the list here at the surgery.'

As she drove towards the first of the house calls Libby had to pass the school and on seeing that the children were all out in the yard, on impulse she stopped the car and went to see if Toby was anywhere to be seen so that she could report back to Nathan.

Sure enough, she saw his fair curly mop bobbing up and down as he chased around with another child of similar age, showing no signs of reluctance to be there.

He'd seen her standing outside the railings and came running across breathless.

'Are you all right, Toby?' she asked gently.

'Yes, Dr Hamilton,' he gasped. 'I'm having lots of fun.' And off he went to find the other boy that he'd been playing with.

When she got back in the car she dialled the surgery and asked to speak to Nathan. When he came on the line she told him, 'Don't worry about Toby any more. The children were all in the playground when I was going past the school so I stopped the car and went across to see if I could see him. He was fine, running around with another small boy, and came across when he saw me. When I asked if he was all right he said he was having lots of fun.'

There was silence for a moment, then with his voice deepening he said, 'Thanks for that, Libby. It was kind of you to take the trouble.'

'It was no trouble,' she said lightly as if the pair of them weren't in her every waking thought. 'I'll see you later.' And rang off.

* * *

The Pellows were a dysfunctional family who seemed to go from one crisis to another.

Angelina, the mother, was an artist who, when the creative mood was on her, would disappear into her studio for days on end. No shopping would be done or tidying up of the shambolic old house down a lane at the far end of the village where she and her family lived.

Her husband Malik was employed by the forestry commission and during her absences had to do the best he could in looking after their two children and things in general. He didn't complain much because Angelina almost always sold what she'd painted, but there was relief all round when she surfaced again.

The young ones always seemed robust and healthy enough, but not today, it would seem, with regard to one of them. Malik had phoned to ask for a visit to six-year-old Ophelia, who had recently been diagnosed with measles and now had a high temperature, was very dizzy, and was complaining that her ears hurt.

When Libby arrived at the house she found that another of Angelina's disappearances was in progress and Malik was busy making a lunch of sorts for him and the child, who was lying on a sofa in the sitting room.

When she examined her ears with an otoscope it was evident that the eardrums were swollen and when she asked the little girl where they hurt she pointed weepily to the area where her cheekbone met the inner ear.

'I suspect that Ophelia has got viral labyrinthitis,' Libby told her father. 'It's an infection of the middle ear that affects balance and makes the ears quite painful. It sometimes occurs when measles is present and can

take some time to clear. There are two kinds of the illness, viral and bacterial. Viral is the less serious of the
two but not to be ignored by any means.

'Your daughter needs to rest, and I'm going to prescribe a low-dosage antihistamine course of treatment
because of her age, and an equally mild children's pain-
relief tablet.

'I see that the measles rash has disappeared so that
problem is obviously lessening. It's unfortunate that in
its wake has come labyrinthitis. Ring the surgery if any
further problems appear, Malik, and I'll come straight
away.'

She looked around her at the cluttered sitting room.
'Do I take it that Angelina isn't available?'

'Yes, you do,' he said morosely. 'She's having one of
her artistic sabbaticals that can go on for days or even
weeks.'

A vision of his wife as she'd last seen her came to
mind, dressed in a golden kaftan with beads and ban-
gles everywhere, and Libby hid a smile.

Angelina had looked more like a fortune teller than
an artist.

The rest of the house calls were soon dealt with and
as she drove back to the practice Libby stopped for a
few moments beside the lake that was only a short distance from the surgery, a stretch of water that was so
beautiful it always took her breath away. The white sails
of yachts were outlined vividly against its calm waters,
and a house built from the pale grey stone of the area
was clearly visible on a tree-covered island in the centre of it.

Above the lake the fells towered in rugged magnificence, but all those who lived in the area knew that they could be dangerous too, that they sometimes asked a grim price from those who loved to climb them. The mountain rescue services were kept busy all the year round on behalf of those caught in bad weather up on the tops, or with others who lacked the experience to stay safe while climbing them.

Nathan had been involved in mountain rescue when he'd lived in Swallowbrook before. An experienced climber, he'd often been called out when the need had arisen, but she couldn't see that happening now, not with Toby to care for. It was often a risky undertaking bringing to safety those who had succumbed to the dangers of the fells, and poor Toby had already been orphaned once.

As she pointed the car homewards it was a strange feeling to know that when she arrived back at the surgery he would be there, closeted in the consulting room that had been his father's, and along with Hugo further along the corridor would be dealing with the afternoon surgery until, in a matter of minutes, it would be time for him to pick Toby up from school.

As she was about to take his place he said, 'It is so good to be back here at the practice, Libby. You have no idea how much I missed it while I was away.' She stared at him disbelievingly. 'What? Do you think I don't mean it?'

'I'm not sure,' she replied. 'Once you'd gone to Africa you never came back to visit, did you, and you were eager enough to be gone in the first place?'

It was a moment to tell her that he had come back all right, but no one had known about it, and the memory of seeing her as a bride smiling up at Jefferson surfaced from the dark corners of his mind once again. The frustration and dismay of that catastrophic dash halfway across the world to hear from her own lips that Libby had put behind her the hurt he'd caused her was something he wasn't likely to forget.

So it was just the practice that he'd missed, she thought bleakly, not any of those he'd left behind— certainly not her.

But she hadn't waited, had she? She'd done a stupid thing during the long empty weeks after his departure. Let the feeling of rejection that he'd been responsible for cause her to make a wrong decision that had been second only in foolishness to letting herself fall in love with him. They had been two great errors of judgement and she wasn't going to let there be a third.

During that first day of his return they had spoken mainly about practice matters, but Libby had been so aware of him she'd felt relieved when he'd finished for the day and gone to pick Toby up from school.

When she arrived home at a much later hour she was hoping to be able to go in, shut her door and relax with no further sightings of him. It had seemed that her wish might be granted until a ring on the bell when Swallowbrook was bathed in autumn gloaming had her tensing.

It reminded her of the night of his arrival as she went

slowly to the door, and sure enough it was her new neighbour standing in the shadowed porch.

'I know you must have seen enough of me for one day,' he said apologetically, 'but on the point of going to sleep Toby has just told me that it's the harvest festival at the school tomorrow morning and he's expected to take something, and I haven't got anything that would be suitable.'

'Yes,' she said steadily. 'It is the usual procedure for the school children at harvest-time. They bring fruit, vegetables, flowers, and the person who has been chosen to receive their gifts presents them with a harvest loaf, fashioned in the shape of a sheaf of corn. There is a short service afterwards and then they go to their classrooms.'

'I see,' he said slowly. 'I do wish he'd told me sooner.'

'Not to worry,' she told him with the feeling that the fates were not playing fair. They were determined that she wasn't going to avoid Nathan's presence in her life again. 'I have a tree in my back garden that's loaded with apples, and next to it a plum tree burdened likewise.

'If you'd like to come back when I've had my meal and bring a ladder, we should be able to solve your problem.' *But it won't go any way to solving mine,* she thought glumly.

He was smiling. 'Thanks for the suggestion. So far I'm making the grade with Toby, but it wouldn't have gone down too well if he'd been the only kid without something for the harvest, and with regard to your evening meal have you started preparing it?'

She shook her head. 'Not so far. I'm going to have a shower first to wash away the germs of the day from the practice, but I know what I'm having and it won't take long to prepare.'

'And what is that?'

'An omelette, some crusty bread and a glass of wine.'

'I'm quite good with omelettes and I've got the wine, so if you'll bring the bread I'll have a meal ready for us both by the time you come out of the shower. It's the least I can do if you're going to get me off the hook with the harvest. How long before you'll be ready?'

'Er, twenty minutes,' she replied weakly, with the feeling that she was being manipulated and ought to refuse the gesture.

He was turning on his heel. 'All right, Libby. I'll see you then.' And off he went, back to where Toby was sleeping, totally innocent of being the cause of any embarrassment to him.

Libby didn't linger under the shower. In the stipulated time she needed to dry her hair and brush it into some semblance of order, apply some make-up, and find something in her wardrobe that would put the finishing touches to her appearance.

She chose an attractive summer dress of soft blue cotton that clung to her slender curves in all the right places, but as she was on the point of zipping it up the voice of reason was asking, Are you insane? Dressing up for the man who gave you the brush-off all that time ago and is showing no signs of having changed his mind? You need old jeans and a cotton top for climbing ladders and getting the message over that the days of you wanting him are long gone.

So old jeans it was and an average T-shirt to go with them and off she went, carrying the bread that she'd bought at the bakery in her lunch hour.

The table was set and he was on the point of taking the first omelette out of the pan, so she quickly buttered the bread and at his request poured the wine, and all the time she was wishing that she'd kept to her first intention and dressed up for the impromptu meal that they were about to share, especially as Nathan was attired in the smart casual clothes that she'd seen him in once before and been much impressed.

If she had expected awkward silences as the meal progressed she was mistaken. As if he was geared up for no embarrassment, his conversation was all about the practice, Swallowbrook and the coming harvest, and when he asked who was going to be there to receive the children's gifts she said, 'It's me, I'm afraid. The headmaster decided that as so many of the children and their parents already know me from the surgery it would be nice if I could spare the time.

'I would have refused if it had been later in the day, but it will only be for the first half-hour or so in the morning and Hugo is going to hold the fort until I show up. Also you're due at the surgery at half past nine if I'm delayed for any reason.'

'Yes, of course,' he said evenly, aware that she was still putting up a cold front as far as he was concerned.

When they'd finished eating and tidied the kitchen Nathan said, 'While I'm getting the ladder out, would you mind popping upstairs to check on Toby? He sometimes wakens up crying for his mother.'

'And what do you do when that happens?' she asked anxiously.

'Hold him close until the moment has passed and he has gone back to sleep. Understandably there were a lot of those kind of moments when he first came to me, but they are gradually reducing and since coming to Swallowbrook there hasn't been one.'

'Have you any regrets about taking on such a big responsibility?' she asked gently, because when it came to what he'd done for Toby she could find no fault in him and had to fight the desire to help him in every way she could.

But Nathan wasn't asking for her help. She would die of mortification if she offered it and he turned her down in the same way as when she'd offered him her heart.

'No, none,' he said in answer to her question. 'If ever I have any children of my own, he will be as one of them to me. Nothing will change my love for him, and he's brought purpose into my life.'

He was capable of great love, she thought bleakly. One day some fortunate woman would come along and she would be truly blessed if he should give his heart to her.

'Shall we start picking the fruit?' she asked, bringing back to mind her suggestion for solving his predicament regarding the harvest. 'I have a safety light at the back of the cottage, which will help us to see in the dark.'

He nodded. 'I'll go up the ladder and throw the fruit

down to you. Do you want me to take it all off for you, or just enough for Toby to take to the school?'

'All of it, I think, if you don't mind,' she told him. 'I have a large basket that will hold the apples and a big earthenware dish for the plums.'

They were making good progress with the fruit-picking. She was actually enjoying it, Libby was thinking, in spite of the awkwardness she felt in his company, but there was about to be an interruption.

His phone was ringing next door and, jumping off the ladder, he said, 'I need to get that fast before it disturbs Toby.' He ran towards his place. 'I won't be long, Libby.'

When he'd gone she stood around for a few moments and then decided that she may as well go up the ladder and carry on where he'd left off. Engrossed in what she was doing, she didn't see him come back into the shadowed garden until he called up to her. Taken by surprise, she turned swiftly and the ladder, propped against the tree trunk, moved with her, tilting backwards and throwing her off.

In those few seconds she was expecting to land on a flagged patio beneath the trees, but she was reckoning without his quick thinking. Instead of hitting the ground, she found herself safe in his arms with her fast-beating heart close against his chest.

'Wow,' he said softly as he looked down at her. 'Why didn't you wait until I came back?' Their glances met. 'But that's not how you do things, is it?'

She was too shocked for the meaning behind his

words to register. Instead she was thinking that he had only ever touched her twice in all the years she'd known him and both times it had been out of necessity rather than desire.

The first time had been at the airport when an intended peck on the cheek in the form of an apology for his harshness had somehow become a moment of passion, and tonight it had been when he'd saved her from what could have been a nasty fall, and now with her still held close in his arms he was carrying her inside and placing her on the sofa in her sitting room.

'Are you all right after that scare?' he asked, looking down at her anxiously.

'Yes, I'm fine. Just a bit shaken, that's all,' she assured him, which was true, but it was more due to where she'd found herself when she'd been saved from harm, rather than being thrown off the ladder.

He was frowning. 'I'm going to have to go, Libby. I've left Toby alone for long enough, but I do need to know that you're all right. He sleeps in my room at present, so I do have a spare room and a camp bed. Do you want to come and spend the night with us so that my mind will be at rest about you?

'I'll move Toby and I into the spare and you can have my room. I might have caught you, but the suddenness of it could have jarred every bone in your body and it doesn't always take effect immediately.'

She could feel her colour rising. A night under the same roof as him would have been very appealing at one time but not now, because if she ever came as close to him again as she'd been when he'd caught her she wouldn't be able to guarantee keeping to her vows of staying clear of him, and that was already beginning to look like a no-no, as try as she would to avoid him he was invading her evenings as well as her days.

'Thanks for the offer, but I really will be fine,' she told him, 'and do, please, go back to Toby. I can't bear the thought of him wakening and you not being there.'

He nodded. 'OK. I'll go, but ring me if you have any problems in the night and we'll both come over.'

'Don't forget to take Toby some of the fruit for the harvest,' she reminded him with a change of subject, pointing to a small wicker basket on the coffee table beside her. 'If you put it in that, it shouldn't be too heavy for him to carry.'

He did as she'd suggested without speaking and when it was done wished her goodnight and departed.

When he'd gone she sat gazing out into the dark night with her mind in a whirl. So he thought she didn't need him, which was not surprising as she was giving him no reason to think otherwise. She was putting on a good show of indifference, false as it was, because after being in his arms and held so close to him she was realising that it was no use pretending any more. She needed him like she needed to breathe, but Nathan was never going to know that.

He'd humiliated her once, a second time was not to be endured, and as her neck started to ache from the jarring of the fall and a headache was coming on she went upstairs to bed and wished she'd accepted his offer if only to be around when Toby awoke the next morning.

Back at the cottage next door Nathan was also facing up to what he saw as home truths. One of them being that Libby still hadn't forgiven him for past hurts, and another was that she was only tolerating his presence because of Toby who she was so sorry for, and saw himself merely as part of the package.

But he could wait for that forgiveness. Make it up to her somehow. Ever since that day in the church porch he'd been cultivating patience, along with the strength of will that had helped him to give her breathing space after Jefferson had died.

He would have stayed away if it hadn't been for the needs of one small boy. Still, one day he might find the right moment to tell Libby how sorry he was for the way he'd treated her at the airport that day, but with her on the defensive all the time it might be some time in coming.

CHAPTER FOUR

THE next morning Nathan kept a lookout for Libby going across to open the surgery at eight o'clock in preparation for the eight-thirty start, as was her routine. He'd decided that if she didn't appear he would be round at the cottage next door immediately to check up on her, but not until then because he felt that in his eagerness to have her under his roof the night before he might have overdone it.

He would be concerned for anyone who had escaped what could have been a very serious fall and might be suffering from the after-effects of the incident, but this was Libby, blonde, beautiful and the most caring person he'd ever known. He was really getting to know her at last and liking it more than he could have ever believed he would.

He'd only moved away from the window for a moment to give Toby his cereal and when he turned back she was there, crossing the short distance that separated the two cottages from the practice building, wearing a blue dress that enhanced her golden fairness and clung to her slender curves as if it was moulded on them.

It was very different from the plain suits she wore

during surgery hours, but she was doing the harvest thing this morning and must have decided that the children should see her in something less sombre while she was in their midst.

As far as he could see, she seemed all right after the night before, and if where she'd landed had not been to her liking she had concealed it very well.

Hugo had just arrived and as the two doctors met at the main doors of the surgery and chatted for a moment Nathan thought how relaxed she was with him, smiling at something he'd said and showing no signs of the guarded approach that she reserved for himself.

Presumably the other man had done nothing to upset her, which was more than could be said for his treatment of her. But now he was back where he belonged, amongst the lakes and fells, working in the practice once more, and with those things to provide some small degree of togetherness he was really getting to know Libby Hamilton who for as long as he could remember had always been on the edges of his life and was now filling it with all the things he'd ever wanted in a woman.

Unaware that she was being observed, Libby hesitated for a moment when Hugo had gone into the building and glanced across at his place.

What was she thinking? he wondered.

He was soon to find out. She was retracing her steps back to the cottages and coming up his path. When she knocked on the door he was there in an instant, observing her questioningly.

'I've just been to open up at the surgery,' she explained, 'and thought I'd call back to let you know that I'm fine after our fruit-picking episode. No harm done.'

'That's good,' he said, and had to step to one side before he could say anything else as Toby was behind him, wanting to speak to Dr. Hamilton.

As she smiled at the child she said, 'It is rather a mouthful for Toby to have to say every time he refers to me. Can't he just call me Libby?'

'Yes, if you are happy with that,' he agreed, 'though maybe not this morning in front of the whole school.'

'No, perhaps not, but after that it will be fine,' she told him, and wished they could have a conversation that sounded less stiff and formal.

But at least he was there in the flesh, she could see him, touch him if she so desired, but *desire* was not the name of the game where they were concerned. Just because he'd held her close in his arms the night before, it didn't mean that Nathan had any yearnings in that direction.

'I have to go,' she said with sudden urgency. 'I've arranged to see a patient before I go to the school. Patrice Lewis is Hugo's sister. Do you remember me telling you that he left a position in general practice in one of the southern counties to help her through a difficult time?

'She lost her husband round about the same time that Ian died and has been left with two young girls to bring up. She is very gentle and can't always cope with her grief, so Hugo has come to join her for as long as it takes for her to get back onto an even footing.

'I see her once a month for a chat and a repeat of any medication she may be on, and her appointment, which she relies on a lot, was made before I was asked to take part in the harvest celebration at the school. So once she has been I'll see you both there, won't I?'

As she hurried back to the surgery Libby was wishing she hadn't ended that last sentence with a question. It had overtones of pleading and that was the last thing she was ever going to do where he was concerned.

The school hall was full when she arrived, with the primary classes at the front, the junior school behind them, and any parents who had been free to attend seated at the back.

Toby was on the front row, clutching his basket of fruit, and as she took her seat on the platform they exchanged smiles. She'd given up on trying not to care for him too much. How could she not allow herself to want to see a small boy happy?

Sitting at the back, Nathan had seen those smiles and she would have been surprised to know that his thoughts were running along similar lines. That if Libby could show Toby the love and tenderness that he was missing from his mother, maybe the sad gap in his young life might be filled. She was living next door to them and except for actually residing in the same house, she couldn't be much closer to the child than that.

He knew that she had none of those kinds of feelings for *him*. Would take a dim view of the way his thoughts were racing ahead. But it was early days, and time was on his side. He and the boy weren't going anywhere and hopefully neither was she.

* * *

Libby and the headmaster were seated behind a long wooden table covered with a white cloth and as the children were helped up onto the platform one by one she accepted the gifts they had brought with a smile for each one of them.

When the last one had handed over their harvest offering she placed her own contribution, a large crusty loaf baked in the shape of a sheaf of corn, in the middle of them, and then a short service of thanksgiving took place.

She saw Nathan leave the hall just before half past nine and remembered her comment to him that if she wasn't back by then she would expect him to be there assisting Hugo with the first surgery of the day.

What did he think of her behind his politely pleasant manner? she wondered. That she was a dried-up, widowed, boss woman, and an unforgiving one at that? The thought brought tears to her eyes. It wasn't how she wanted him to see her, but it was one way of hiding her feelings.

As he'd walked back to the practice with the vision of her on the platform in the blue dress at the front of his mind, Nathan had been thinking that it was as well that Libby had been wearing her old clothes the night before when he'd caught her in his arms, or he might have forgotten that he was supposed to be keeping to their lukewarm reunion and let his awakening consciousness of her ruin everything.

As the golden days of autumn dwindled, with winter's chill hovering late at night and in the pale dawn, he said one morning, 'Is it all right with you if I call everyone at the practice together to make an announcement before the day gets under way, Libby?'

'Yes, of course,' she replied, with dread making her feel nauseous at the thought of what he might be about to say, such as that he was moving on to somewhere new, for which she could be responsible with her lack of welcome and aloofness.

When Nathan had first come back to Swallowbrook he'd been emphatic that it was there he wanted to be, but when he'd said that he hadn't been expecting to find himself living next door to an ice maiden.

When they were all assembled in the practice manager's office he said, 'Just a quick word. As I came back to Swallowbrook almost at the same time as my father was retiring from the practice, I wasn't able to arrange a suitable farewell for him, so I am going to put that right on Saturday evening by inviting you all to a meal in the banqueting suite of the new hotel by the lakeside.'

As relief washed over her Libby's colour was rising. Before anyone else had the chance to reply she said, 'I would like to make it clear that *we* didn't get the opportunity to do something like that when your father left us because he was adamant that he would want you to be there on the occasion of anything of that nature, so we had to leave it in order to abide by his wishes.

'I for one will be delighted to accept the invitation. John Gallagher was more to me than just a colleague, he was there for me always in the good times and bad.' Her voice broke. *'He cared, and caring is a precious thing.'*

There was silence for a moment then everyone began to talk at once, expressing their pleasure at being asked to such a gathering. For the rest of the day the surprise party was the main topic of conversation when anyone had a free moment.

As Libby had gone back to her consulting room Nathan had been close behind and he'd followed her inside and closed the door.

'There was no criticism intended in what I said, Libby. I know what Dad can be like when he digs his heels in,' he told her. 'You wanting to arrange a farewell must have coincided with me getting in touch with him to say that I was coming back with my soon-to-be-adopted son. I presume he didn't pass that information on because I'd been away so long, he felt that he would believe it when he saw it.'

She was smiling. 'I think what you are arranging is a lovely idea. You are making up for the lack of a proper farewell and that is all that matters, yet what about Toby? It will be late for him to be up.'

He nodded. 'Yes, I know, but there is no one I can leave him with that I would trust, except you.'

'I wouldn't mind if you want me to stay behind with him.'

'Maybe you wouldn't, but I would, and Dad will be most upset if you aren't there. Also Toby and Grandfather Gallagher, as he calls my father, are getting on famously. I shall book a room for the night and when he gets tired tuck him up safely in there and keep checking on him every so often.'

'I could do that for you,' she suggested, 'so that you don't have to leave your guests.'

'So shall I book a room for you as well?'

'Yes, why not?' she agreed. 'It will be nice to have a leisurely breakfast that someone else has prepared overlooking the lake on the Sunday morning.'

'I can agree with that wholeheartedly,' he said, and went to start his day, leaving her to greet her first patient with a lighter heart than she'd had for some time. *Nathan wanted her to be at the party, she thought. She didn't know why exactly. Maybe it was just because of her position in the practice. Whatever it might be, it was like balm to her soul because for the first time since widowhood had fallen on her she would be attending a social event and he would be there.*

Laura Standish and her husband had been wanting to start a family for quite some time but without success due to her irregular menstrual cycle and his low sperm count, but today it was a different story. When she seated herself opposite Libby the reason for her consulting a doctor became clear.

She explained tremulously that she was experiencing all the signs of early pregnancy and was desperate for confirmation from a reliable source.

'I feel nauseous in the mornings,' she said, 'my breasts are tender, and I've missed two periods. I know I'm irregular, Libby, but I've never missed two full months before.'

'Have you done a pregnancy test from the chemist?' she asked.

Laura shook her head. 'No. I preferred to come to you for the good or bad news. We'd got to the point where the gynaecologist you sent us to was suggesting IVF treatment. Then suddenly, almost like a miracle, I feel as if I might be pregnant.'

'Shall we see if you're right?' Libby told her gently, pointing to the couch beside them.

When she'd finished the test and examination that would confirm whether her patient's dearest wish was to be granted she shook her head. 'I'm sorry, Laura,' she told her, 'not this time, I'm afraid. It is more likely to be a hormone imbalance. Maybe you should give IVF some thought the next time you see the gynaecologist.'

'Why is it that it is so easy for some people to have a baby and so difficult for others?' Laura said tearfully. 'Mike will be so disappointed.'

'Nature is a law unto itself and can be very cruel sometimes,' she told her with the memory of a teenage girl that she'd seen the day before who had been desperate to terminate an unwanted pregnancy that had been the result of her one and only venture into unprotected sex.

The first delivery of the flu prevention vaccine had arrived, so it turned out to be an extremely busy day for the practice nurses, with the waiting room full of a mixture of those waiting for the jab and the ones who'd just been given it hanging on for the suggested twenty minutes before leaving the premises in case they suffered any ill effects, and alongside them those who were waiting to consult their doctor about other things.

That being so, it was evening before Libby was able to take her mind back to Nathan's surprise announcement at the start of the day. The party was going to be something to look forward to, a pleasant surprise, and with that thought in mind what was she going to wear?

It would be an occasion for being neither over-dressed or understated, something in the middle maybe. Avoiding the clothes she'd worn during her brief depressing marriage to Ian, she decided that it was going to be a black dress with long sleeves, low neck and calf-length full skirt, with appropriate jewellery.

Next door Nathan's thoughts were also about the party but along different lines. He and Libby would be sleeping beneath the same roof for once, he was thinking, not the golden thatch above them as he would have liked on the night when Libby had fallen off the ladder, but the roof of a smart new hotel by the lake.

On the Saturday night he went on ahead to the party venue with Toby so as to be there beside his father as he greeted his guests, and to make sure that all was in order with the arrangements he'd made with the hotel.

Hugo was the first to arrive with his sister, who he'd brought along for company, a childminder having been engaged to look after her little girls. Then came the surgery nurses Robina, Tracey and Coleen with their partners, followed by the receptionists also suitably escorted, and tagging along behind them was Gordon, a confirmed bachelor.

Next to arrive was Alison, the cleaner, and her husband, who looked after the gardens around the surgery and did general maintenance on the building when necessary. Even the man from the pathology lab who came each day to collect blood samples for testing and anything else that had to go to his department was there. He'd been coming for so many years he was looked on as one of them. The last, but not the least by any means, was Libby, stunning in black, smiling her pleasure to be there and taking in the vision of Nathan and his father resplendent in dinner jackets, evening shirts and bow-ties. Even Toby was wearing a short-sleeved shirt with a little tie held in place by elastic.

As each guest had arrived John had shaken hands with them cordially until Libby had appeared and then it was different.

He held her close for a long moment and then said gruffly, 'I'm missing you, Libby. How's it going with Nathan back in harness?'

The man in question was only inches away, observing her with an ironic gleam in his eyes as if daring her to be truthful and admit that she was putting up with him on sufferance.

He was in for a surprise. 'Everything at the practice is fine,' she told his father. 'The patients are delighted to see Nathan back, and the rest of us really appreciate his contribution to the village's health care.'

'That's good,' the older man said, and with a glance at Toby, who was looking around him with interest, 'You won't have much time for anything else with the job and this young fellow to look after, eh, Nathan?'

'It would depend on what it was and how important,' he said evenly, with his glance still on her, and now there was no irony in it, just a question that she didn't know the answer to.

By the time the last course of the meal was being served Toby was ready for sleep, nodding his curly blond head every few seconds, and as she observed him Libby said to Nathan in a low voice, 'You can't very well leave your guests, Nathan. Shall I take Toby and get him settled for the night, if he'll let me?'

'I don't think he'll object,' he replied. 'He likes you, Libby, and would be round at your place every minute of the day if I let him.'

'So why don't you?'

'I'm not sure. Maybe it's because I know that I'm not welcome and I wouldn't want that sort of feeling to wash off onto him.'

As she bristled with indignation beside him he said, 'We'd better take him up now before he falls off his chair.'

'Yes,' she agreed, 'but don't think that by hustling me off with Toby, what you have just said about not being welcome is going to pass without comment.'

He was on his feet and didn't reply. Lifting Toby up into his arms, he whispered in his ear, 'Libby is going to give you your bedtime cuddles tonight—is that all right?'

'Mmm,' he murmured.

When they reached the top of the hotel's wide staircase and turned into the first corridor he pointed to two rooms overlooking the lake and, giving her the keys, said, 'The nearest one is yours, and the one next to it is a twin-bedded for Toby and I. When you've opened the door I'll lay him on his bed and then go back to the others, if that's all right with you.'

'Yes,' she whispered. 'I won't come down until I'm sure that he's fast asleep.'

The moment Nathan had gone Toby opened his eyes and smiled up at her drowsily. 'We need to take your shirt and tie off and put your pyjamas on before you go to sleep,' she told him gently. 'They are here beside you where Uncle Nathan has left them, so if you'll just sit up for a moment we'll put them on.'

He did as she'd asked and gazing around him said, 'I haven't got my comforter, Libby,' and with his bottom lip trembling went on, 'I always hold it close when I'm in my bed.'

'What is it, Toby?' she asked as tears began to flow.

'It is Mummy's nightdress, Libby,' he sobbed. 'It's soft and cuddly and smells lovely.'

She was looking around her desperately, lifting the lid of a small overnight case only to find it empty, checking that the nightdress wasn't tangled up in the bedclothes, opening drawers, all to no avail.

'I think that it must have been forgotten when your uncle was packing your things,' she said consolingly, 'but do you know what, Toby? I have a nightdress that smells nice. You can cuddle up to that if you like, pretend that it's your comforter just for tonight. What do you say?'

'Where is it?' he wanted to know.

'In my room next door.' Not wanting to leave him even for a second after watching his distress, she said, 'Shall we go and get it?'

He nodded, and swinging his small legs over the side of the bed took her hand in his and side by side they went to find the nightdress that was folded neatly on her pillow.

She gave it to him and holding it close to his cheek he said, 'Mummy won't mind, will she?'

'No, of course not,' she told him reassuringly. 'She will be happy that you are happy. So if that is all right, shall we go and tuck you up in bed?'

The room that Nathan had booked for her had a double bed in it and as Toby observed it he said, 'Can I sleep in your bed, Libby?'

The thought of having him safe and close beside her was tempting, and what the outcome would be if she left him asleep in the next room and when she'd gone to join the others he awoke in the distressed state he'd been in earlier didn't bear thinking of, so she said, 'Yes, you can, but first I must write a note for someone who loves you very much to tell him where you are when the party is over.'

'You mean Uncle Nathan, don't you? He is going to be my new daddy, did you know that?'

'Yes, he told me how excited he is to be your new dad,' she told him.

Picking up a pen off a nearby writing desk, she wrote on headed notepaper...

Nathan.
Toby is sleeping with me after a major upset that
has now been sorted. It's why I didn't come back

to join the party. I know you will want to see for
yourself that he is all right, so will leave my door
unlocked until you've been and checked on him.
   Libby.

When she'd placed it on Toby's empty pillow in
the next room she took him to her bed and held him
close until he was asleep, then, bereft of her nightwear,
slipped off the dress and lay beside him in the black
lacy slip that she'd worn beneath it.

Down below Nathan was watching the staircase as
coffee was being served to his guests, expecting Libby
to appear any moment, but she didn't materialise and
knowing how tired Toby had been he was wondering
why.

He was tempted to go and check on them but didn't
want to be seen as fussing, either by her or by the surgery staff who were in no hurry to go. But at last they
had all said their farewells and he'd seen his father
safely into a taxi, so was free to go to the suites above
to see where Libby had got to.

The first thing that registered was that there was no
Toby in the bed that he had laid him on. The second
was the note on the pillow. As he read it his expression tightened. For God's sake! What kind of upset was
Libby referring to? Then he was out in the corridor and
pushing back the door that she'd left unlocked.

When he looked inside his face softened. His adopted
son was asleep in the crook of the arm of the woman he
could once have had if he hadn't been too blind to see
what had been under his nose.

As he looked down at the smooth skin of her shoulders inside the flimsy slip and the rise and fall of her breasts as she slept beside the precious child who had been catapulted into his life, it was his turn to fight back the tears for the waste of the years and the mistakes that both of them had made.

He hadn't a clue what could have upset Toby to such an extent until he looked at what he was holding in his arms and as he observed it he gave a hollow groan. He'd forgotten to pack Toby's comforter. How could he have done such a thing? Thank God, Libby had come up with a solution.

His exclamation of dismay must have disturbed her. She had opened her eyes and was looking up at him.

'Everything is all right,' she whispered, and easing her arm from beneath the sleeping child she slid her legs over the side of the bed and stood before him.

'I can't believe that I forgot his comforter, of all things,' he said wretchedly, 'and lumbered you with the aftermath of my carelessness.'

'Stop berating yourself,' she told him. 'You are marvellous to do what you do for Toby. He has told me that you are going to be his new daddy and seems fine with the idea. Forgetting to bring his mummy's nightdress isn't going to change that.'

He was not to be consoled. 'You must wish me a thousand miles away, Libby,' he said bleakly. 'I went out of your life a long time ago and have had the nerve to come bursting back into your planned existence as if by divine right.'

She took a step forward and touched his face with

gentle hands and suddenly nothing else mattered except themselves, not Toby sleeping contentedly beside them, the party that she'd seen little of or the practice that was their daytime rendezvous. There was peace between them for a few brief moments with no recriminations or hurts to spoil it, no bitterness or past mistakes hovering over them. It was a moment of supreme need with desire ruling their emotions.

For the third time in Libby's life Nathan was touching her and there was nothing casual about it this time. His mouth on hers was demanding, urgent, and she was responding with every fibre of her being.

He took her hand and drew her towards the door of a small sitting room at the end of the bedroom and once inside turned the catch to prevent Toby walking in on them. Then he was slipping the black slip off her shoulders and kissing the cleft between her breasts.

As their passion increased Nathan lowered her onto a sofa and as she gazed up at him in the moment before the climax of their desire Libby came to her senses.

She'd already made one big mistake where Nathan was concerned, she thought. This could be another. This wild abandonment of common sense could lead to more heartbreak if she let it continue.

He felt her change of mood as painfully as if it was a knife thrust and as she got slowly to her feet he placed the keys of the suite next door in her hand and said sombrely, 'You can't let go of the past, can you, Libby?

'If you don't mind swapping I'll take over here and we'll see you at breakfast. Do you need to take anything with you?'

'Just the things I brought with me for an overnight stay,' she said weakly, and flinging her belongings into her travel bag she wrapped herself in the robe that she'd brought with her and went.

So much for that, he thought grimly when she'd gone. He'd lost the control that he'd been cultivating ever since coming back to Swallowbrook and all because Libby had stroked his face. Yet it hadn't been just that, had it?

His emotions had already run amok when he'd discovered he'd left Toby's comforter behind and Libby had been left to handle the distress that the oversight had caused his little one, and when instead of blame she'd shown him only tenderness the barriers between them had come down.

He'd given in to passion she'd aroused in him and blown it, had been able to tell that the change in her response to his love-making had been because she'd suddenly remembered how he had once let her see that he wasn't interested in any feelings she might have for him, and had told her cruelly to go and forget him.

It had seemed as if she'd taken him at his word when she'd married Jefferson, and he'd stayed away even after he'd died and Libby was free of him, because of what he'd said that day. Was the awful mistake he'd made always going to be there to haunt him?

As Toby stirred in his sleep and held Libby's nightdress more closely to him, Nathan eased himself carefully onto the bed beside him in the place where she had lain and wondered what tomorrow would bring in a relationship that seemed to be going nowhere.

He'd come back to Swallowbrook with no intentions

towards Libby other than telling her, if she would give him the chance, how much he regretted the way he'd behaved that day at the airport when her timing had been so unfortunate.

CHAPTER FIVE

WHEN Libby went down to breakfast the following morning, pale and drawn after a sleepless night, Nathan and Toby were already seated at a table by a window overlooking the lake on the point of finishing theirs.

When Toby called across to her she had no choice but to go to where Nathan was observing her unsmilingly from the opposite side of the table.

She didn't want to sit with them, the happenings of the night before were too recent, too raw, but she could tell that Toby was expecting her to and there was no way she wanted to upset him. So she asked Nathan, 'Is it all right if I join you?'

'Yes, of course,' he said evenly, and she thought that the core of their relationship, *if it could be described as that*, was as past its promise as the fallen leaves of bronze and gold lying beneath the trees that surrounded the lake.

The mellow autumn of Nathan's return to Swallowbrook was past, winter would soon be upon them and where she'd always looked forward to crisp mornings and snow on the fells, this time it was going to be an ordeal to be got through.

A waitress was at her elbow, asking if she was ready to order, and bringing herself back from the gloom of her thoughts Libby consulted the menu.

When she had gone Nathan asked, as if nothing between them had changed, 'Are you staying here for the rest of the day or checking out, like Toby and I?'

'I intend leaving immediately after breakfast,' she told him. 'There are things I have to do when I get back—household chores, paperwork from the surgery to look through, and other matters to attend to.' She made an attempt at a smile. 'I take it that everyone enjoyed the party?'

'Yes, it appeared so, *except for the two of us.* Maybe you will let me make it up to you at some time in the future? I owe you that.'

'You don't owe me anything,' she said in a low voice that was not for Toby's ears. 'I suggest we forget last night.'

'Just like that?' he said evenly. 'It would seem that you have a very low pain threshold.'

'All hurts lessen in time,' she replied, and as the waitress returned with the food that she'd ordered the stressful conversation dwindled into silence.

Nathan got to his feet and said, 'Come along, Toby, say goodbye to Libby.' He looked at her. 'We'll return your emergency "comforter" when it has been washed and ironed. Thanks again for the loan of it.'

She put down her knife and fork and observing him gravely commented, 'I was only too happy to be of use *with regard to that,*' and to Toby who was looking around him, unaware of the undercurrents between them, she said, 'I'll see you soon, Toby. Do I get a kiss?'

'Mmm,' he said, and pursing his lips placed them against her cheek.

As the two of them went out into the car park Nathan thought wryly that it was nice to know that one of them was in favour.

If ever the day dawned when Libby was ready to wipe the slate clean he would feel that at last the wheel had turned its full circle for them. At the present time it was just something that only happened in his dreams.

When she went to Reception to settle her account for the suite that she had occupied briefly she was told that it had been paid by Dr Nathan Gallagher.

He was heaping coals of fire on her head, she thought miserably, with the memory of his cool comment that he would return her nightdress when it had been washed, and now she was discovering that Nathan had paid for the luxurious accommodation that she'd had little time to take note of the night before.

The receptionist had noticed that she'd been taken aback, and volunteered the information that the account had been settled the week previously when Dr Gallagher had paid in full for everything that the hotel had arranged to provide, and as she went out to have a last stroll beside the lake she thought wretchedly that she'd been wrong about the 'coals of fire' and should be ashamed. He had treated her as he would any friend or acquaintance. The fact that the night before had escalated into something totally mind-blowing had been down to her as much as him.

As she walked beside the still waters the house on the island that could only be reached by boat came into view. She'd heard recently that it had become a tourist attraction and was available to rent for those who craved solitude in one of the most beautiful settings for miles around.

The next time she had the chance to take a break from the practice she would stay there if it was available, she decided. Where no one or nothing could take away the confidence in herself that had disappeared completely the night before when Nathan had begun to make love to her and the longing that she'd thought was under control had become a bright flame of desire.

During the week after the party Libby and Nathan spoke only briefly about surgery matters and in the evenings stayed well apart, until the night when Toby turned up on her doorstep with the nightdress neatly wrapped and with a note attached to say, 'Thanks again for the loan, Libby. I'm sending it with Toby as I have a strong feeling that my presence would not be welcome. Sorry I can't make myself scarce during surgery hours, Nathan.'

When she'd read it she looked across, knowing that he would be somewhere near, that he would not let Toby out into the wintry dusk even for a second without being nearby. Sure enough, he was standing in the doorway of the cottage next door where he could see him.

'Can I come in, Libby?' the young messenger asked once he'd delivered the package.

'Yes, if it is all right with your uncle,' she said immediately, and called across to ask if he could stay and play for a while.

Nathan nodded. 'Yes, for half an hour and then it will be his bedtime.'

Exactly thirty minutes later she took him back and when he opened the door to them Toby said, 'We've had lots of fun playing hide and seek.'

'Really,' was Nathan's only comment as his young charge skipped past him. Giving in to the urge to get him talking on a more friendly level, she asked, 'What have you got planned for Toby at Christmas?'

'Nothing at the moment,' was the answer. 'Why, have you got any ideas?'

'Er, no, but I could give it some thought. It will be his first Christmas in Swallowbrook and yours after a long gap, so it should be something special.'

'Not necessarily for me,' he said dryly, 'but for Toby, yes, absolutely. We'll probably go to stay with Dad for the two days. What are you planning to do?'

She knew he didn't care a jot about what she would be doing, that he was merely asking out of politeness. Any frail rapport they'd had was gone, blown away as if the cold winds from the fells were already in their winter mode.

'I haven't made any plans as yet,' she told him, 'though I will be somewhere around. This place is too lovely to be away from at Christmastime, or have you forgotten?'

'I forget nothing,' he said levelly. 'Neither the good or the bad,' and she wondered what that was supposed to mean. Maybe it was a hint that the conversation had gone on long enough with her standing on the doorstep like someone trying to sell him something, unwelcome and unwanted.

'I've got things to do so will say goodnight,' she said abruptly, and he didn't protest.

The October half-term at the village school was approaching and Libby was curious to know what arrangements Nathan was going to make regarding it.

Hugo was going to be away that week. He was taking his sister and her children away for a short break, so Nathan wouldn't be asking for time off as the two of them would be needed at the surgery.

She wasn't expecting him to discuss his plans with her as they only ever spoke about surgery matters, apart from the one occasion when she had asked him what he was planning for Christmas and received an evasive answer.

So she was surprised when one morning as they waited for the surgery to start he said, 'I can't make up my mind about the half-term break. Whether I should enrol Toby for the play group they have at the school during holidays for children with working parents, or take Dad up on his offer to have him while I'm here. What would you do if you were me, Libby?'

'I'm not sure,' she told him, concealing her surprise at being asked. 'I imagine that your father would love to have him, but he *was* looking forward to a complete rest after all the years as senior partner here. On the other hand, he might be finding that he has more time on his hands than he wants now, and from Toby's point of view there is the attraction of the river and the fishing.

'But the play group is well organised and well attended and Toby would be with some of his school friends. Why don't you ask him which he would like the best?'

'I know what he'll say to that,' he replied whimsically. 'It will be Grandfather Gallagher and the river. Maybe it won't be too taxing for Dad if you can manage on your own for the first hour in the morning and the last couple of hours at night. Can you, Libby?'

'Yes,' she told him steadily. 'I'll fit in with whatever is best for Toby. Just let me know when you've decided. I'm having a week off myself early next month but Hugo will be back by then and half-term will be over.'

'Are you going away? Or staying local?' he questioned.

'Local, but not too local,' she told him, 'just far enough away to have some time to myself.'

'And you are not going to tell me where?'

'No,' she said equably, and went to start her day at the Swallowbrook practice with a vision of a house on an island that she had arranged to rent for the week.

The morning was progressing like most other mornings at that time of year, a few coughs and sniffles, mixed with patients who were there because they had more serious anxieties to consult their doctors about, and once again there was the gathering of the willing and the unwilling who had come to have their flu jabs.

One of the patients was a young pregnant woman whose baby was almost due. She'd come to the surgery because of severe indigestion and when her name was called she got slowly to her feet.

Libby was standing in the doorway of her consulting room, waiting to usher her inside, when suddenly she let out a scream of pain and clutched herself around the waist.

'I think it's the baby,' she gasped. 'I thought the pains I've been having every so often were indigestion as I'm not due until next week, but this is different.'

'A week too soon is nothing when it is a first baby,' Libby told her, and taking her by the arm drew her quickly inside.

Nathan was saying goodbye to one of his patients at the other end of the corridor that separated their consulting rooms and took in the situation immediately. As she was helping the distressed woman on to the bed nearby he appeared and stood by as she checked to see if it *was* the baby on its way.

'I can see the head already,' she said quickly. 'See for yourself, Nathan.'

He didn't need to be asked twice and when he'd done so asked with low-voiced urgency, 'Have you ever done a delivery before?'

She shook her head. 'I know the procedure but have never had to put it into practice.'

'I have,' he said reassuringly. 'I've done dozens of them where I've been for the last three years. In those kind of places one has to be jack of all trades.' He turned to the anxious woman on the bed. 'It's going to be all right. What is your name?'

'Jodie,' she informed him between cries of pain.

'So try to keep as calm as you can, Jodie,' he said soothingly. 'There isn't going to be time to get you to hospital before the birth, but I'm used to delivering babies, so not to worry.'

'I need to push!' she cried.

'Yes, I know you do,' he told her, 'but if you can wait for just a few seconds until I tell you to, everything is going to be fine. In just a few moments you'll be holding your baby, so can you do that for me?'

'I'll try,' she gasped, and with Libby beside him holding a clean towel that she'd taken from a cupboard by the bed he said, 'Now you can push.'

With a huge heave she did so and seconds later a perfectly formed baby girl was wrapped in the towel and placed into her arms. As the tiny one expanded her lungs with a lusty cry a cheer broke the silence that had settled on the waiting room and the two doctors exchanged smiles.

In the euphoria of the birth Libby was forgetting everything except how the two of them, Nathan and herself, had shared such a special moment. Turning to him, she held him close for a few seconds before he dealt with the removal of the placenta.

'I can see that we are going to have to do this more often if this is what I get,' he said softly as she let her arms fall away. 'If this is how it feels to see someone else's child come into the world, can you imagine what it must be like with one of your own?'

'No, I'm afraid I can't,' she told him flatly as he brought her back down to earth. 'I stopped wishing for the moon a long time ago.'

'Point taken,' he replied in a similar tone, and turned back to the ecstatic new mother.

'Could someone phone my husband to tell him that he has a daughter?' Jodie asked in awed wonder. 'He's the trauma technician based at the fire station in the town centre.'

The ambulance that had been sent for had arrived and Libby said, 'Yes, of course, and we'll tell him that the two of you are on your way to the maternity unit at the hospital.

'Have you chosen a name for the baby?' she asked as mother and child were being transferred to the ambulance a few minutes later.

'Yes,' was the reply. 'When we knew that the baby would be born in October, we chose Octavia for a girl and Octavius for a boy.'

'Very impressive,' Nathan commented briefly when Libby told him the baby's name. He had already gone back to his patients, and she hurried back to hers who had waited with much good humour for the morning surgery to return to normal.

After the moment of euphoria when she'd hugged him to her Libby's upbeat feeling about them continued to dwindle as the day progressed because she kept remembering what he'd said about having children of one's own.

At one time she'd dreamt of having a boy like him, dark-haired, dark-eyed, incredibly handsome, and a girl with blonde hair and the kind of ready smile that she used to have, which now appeared as infrequently as the sun in winter.

But long ago he'd dashed those hopes as casually as if discussing the weather, and Ian's lax approach to marriage had stopped any yearnings in that direction, so if the day ever dawned when she held a child of her own in her arms, it would be the age of miracles.

The arrangements for Toby at half-term turned out as Nathan had expected. John and the river had the vote, with his young visitor even sleeping at the lodge in a small bedroom that the older man had fitted out for him.

It meant that Nathan was able to put in a full day at the practice while the two doctors were holding the fort during Hugo's absence. It also gave him some free time for himself, which he hadn't had much of since taking Toby into his life.

As they left the surgery one evening to go to their respective cottages he said to Libby, 'I don't feel like cooking, so am going to get changed and dine at the hotel where we had Dad's farewell. Do you feel like joining me?'

She hesitated. The thought of a delightful meal in equally delightful surroundings was tempting, but keeping up a front of casual detachment in the place where they had been so drawn to each other wasn't. Yet even as the thought was going through her mind she found herself saying, 'Yes, why not? I don't feel like cooking either. I feel tired and drab, so like you I will go and change into something less formal.'

'The blue dress maybe,' he suggested casually. 'It looked good on you that day at the school harvest.'

'Yes. I suppose it would be suitable,' she told him, concealing her surprise at discovering that he'd remembered what she was wearing on that occasion. But this was Nathan who not so long ago had been quick to point out that there was nothing wrong with *his* memory, as if hers might be at fault!

'How long before you want to go?' she asked, getting back to basics.

'Half an hour?'

'Yes, I'm starving, and, Nathan, I want it to be my shout. I remember finding that my account had been paid when I went to settle it the last time I was there.'

'So? You were my guest.'

She was frowning. 'Even so...'

He sighed. 'Do you recall me saying that I would like to make it up to you for taking up your evening with Toby's problems? So please don't argue, Libby.'

'All right,' she agreed at last. Maybe what had happened between them had been an aberration. A moment of madness that had come out of the blue. Tonight it would be just a matter of two busy doctors unwinding over a pleasant meal. There could be no harm in that.

They were separating at the bottom of their respective drives and as she went upstairs to shower and change, out of the wardrobe came the blue dress.

When she went out to join him wearing it he nodded his approval and for the first time in ages she felt beautiful.

The evening progressed just how she wanted it to

be, friendly and tranquil, with no disturbing vibes to make her feel threatened or on edge as she listened to Nathan describing the traumas and the good times of his time in Africa.

'Was it so demanding that you never had the chance to come back home for a break?' she asked at one point.

There was a pause in what had been a relaxed conversation as his mind went back once again to those soul-destroying moments when he'd stood in the church porch and had to accept that he'd had a wasted journey. He'd been an arrogant fool not to act sooner, to assume that despite their parting words Libby would have continued to have romantic feelings for him and would have waited till he'd come to his senses where she was concerned.

But, no, instead he'd acted on impulse and selfish desire. But he'd got his just deserts. He'd arrived too late to stop the wedding, and as he'd watched her smile up at her new husband had thought that there had been no point in his coming as Libby seemed happy enough with Jefferson.

If he was to tell her that he *had* been home during that time, just the once, what good would it do? She'd loved him once, but not any more, and tonight they were at peace with each other as friends, so why spoil it?

'Yes,' he replied, avoiding her glance. 'The pressures were always too great to be able to take time off.'

As they were about to leave the hotel and he was helping her into the warm jacket that she'd brought with her he asked, 'Do you want to take a stroll by the lake?'

'Yes, if you like,' she told him, with the memory of

that other time when she'd done the same thing alone and in daylight on the morning after the party.

It was then that she'd been attracted to Greystone House, the property on the island, where she was going to stay in a couple of weeks' time.

Tonight it was floodlit with lanterns and so was the lake, like diamonds sparkling on water. When Nathan took her hand in his she didn't draw it out of his clasp, but kept it there, warm and safe, in case she should trip in the semi-darkness.

'What is that place?' he asked, glancing across the water to where the house stood solid and unreachable. 'I remember it from way back but don't ever recall what it was used for.'

'I don't know about then,' she told him, 'but now it is a very popular holiday let, though I'm not sure what degree of the services it has, such as lighting, heating and water, but for anyone wanting peace and solitude it's the perfect place. It's owned by a local businessman who lets it out when his family aren't using it.'

If she told him that she was going to stay there herself in the near future he would think she was crazy no doubt. But it would give her the opportunity to be alone with her thoughts, with the reassurance of knowing that she was just a boat ride away from the things she held dearest.

Every moment spent with Nathan in tranquillity was a joy, but there was always the reminder of things past to spoil it. It was why on the night of his father's party, when she'd been ready to give herself to him completely, she'd backed away. There had been no real closeness between them since then until tonight, just as long as they could keep gentling along like this.

Walking alongside her, still holding her hand, Nathan was thinking the same kind of thoughts. He'd been too pushy that other time and spoilt it, but not tonight. They were in a different mode, though still overwhelmingly aware of each other.

'Is Toby enjoying his stay by the river?' she asked as they went back to where the car was parked on the hotel forecourt.

He was smiling. 'Yes. I don't know which of the two of them is enjoying it the most. Having him around has given Dad something to keep him on his toes, but I have to make sure he isn't doing too much, though Toby isn't a demanding child like some are, and Dad says that he brightens up his life.'

'Becoming his guardian has caused you to have to make many adjustments in yours, hasn't it?' she commented.

'Yes, I have to admit that is so. Before he came to me I was used to doing what suited *me* first and foremost, and now my requirements must always come second. Toby seems happy enough with me, but he needs a mother figure too, which I suppose means that I should find myself a wife.'

He was sounding her out, putting out a feeler to see if she would respond, and she did, but not how he wanted her to.

'I'm sure there will be plenty of applicants for the position once you let that be known,' she replied coolly. 'You have the looks, a beautiful cottage, the job...' *And*

*a heart of stone to be discussing something like this with
me of all people.*

She was averting her gaze from his, didn't see him
flinch, and when he opened the car door for her, she
slid into the passenger seat and stared into the distance.

They were back in the centre of Swallowbrook in
minutes and instead of inviting him in for coffee, as
she had been intending to, Libby thanked him for the
meal, bade him a brief goodnight and was gone, clos-
ing her front door behind her decisively.

Yet there was nothing decisive about the way she
began to climb the stairs with dragging feet and a heavy
heart.

Why couldn't she accept once and for all that Nathan
only wanted her as colleague, neighbour and someone
to play hide and seek with Toby? she thought bleakly.

Throwing off her clothes, she got into bed and wished
that it was tomorrow that she was going to the house on
the island.

She slept at last, only to dream that Nathan was
down below, ringing her doorbell, and when she let
him in he said, 'I love you, Libby, can't live without
you.' But as she moved towards him, smiling with arms
outstretched, she awoke to find that the doorbell *was*
ringing and when she went downstairs he *was* there,
but he wasn't saying the words of her dream. 'Dad has
just phoned to say that Toby is sick,' he said without
preamble. 'I'm going there now and thought I'd better
warn you that I might be missing from the surgery in
the morning.'

'What does he say is wrong with him?' she asked as the doctor in her rose to the surface.

'Temperature, headache, rash—it all sounds worryingly familiar.'

'Meningitis?'

He nodded.

'Give me a couple of minutes to fling on some clothes. I'm coming with you,' she told him.

'Are you sure?'

She was already halfway up the stairs and called down to him, 'Of course I'm sure. Have you got your bag?' He nodded bleakly. 'So go and start the car.'

'When did Toby start to be ill?' she asked as they drove towards the river and his father's lodge.

'Just a short while ago, Dad said. Awoke fretful, poorly, covered in a damned rash and is vomiting. If anything else bad happens to him, I shudder to think how I'll cope,' he said, with his voice thickening, and she thought that love could make strong men weak.

'Nothing *is* going to happen to Toby,' she told him steadily as the complex of retirement homes came into view. 'The two of us, you and I, are not going to let it. We are being given a taste of what it's like for the families of our sick patients. It's the other side of the coin, a lesson to be well learned.'

Toby was how John had described him, but Nathan's father had met them at the door with the news that the rash had come out fully and wasn't the same kind as the symptoms of meningitis. 'My feeling is he's picked up a bug or some sort of virus,' he said as they examined him.

Nathan muttered, 'Thank God it isn't the other thing. This we should be able to cope with, but the problem is I don't know anything about Toby's health before I took him into my care, what or if he had any health problems before I became responsible for him. In normal circumstances parents have firsthand knowledge about anything regarding their child's health.

'I feel pretty sure that his condition this morning is allergy related but am loath to start prescribing anything until someone else has seen him beside ourselves. What do *you* think, Libby?' he asked.

'It could be something he is allergic to,' she agreed, 'but from what to make him so poorly?'

'That's just it, we don't know, do we? It could be from anything—food, toiletries, plants, something airborne.' To Toby, with incredible gentleness, he said, 'Aren't you the lucky one, with three doctors to look after you?'

As she took his hot little hand in hers to feel his pulse he said drowsily, 'When can we play hide and seek again, Libby?'

'Soon,' she soothed, and when she turned round Nathan had been replaced by his father, who said, 'We're not sure what the rash is, are we, Libby? I'm wondering if his condition is due to something that Toby has eaten, and agree with Nathan that we shouldn't prescribe until we are sure what is wrong, which is going to mean taking him to A and E immediately. Do you want to go with them and I'll take the morning surgery for you?'

Daylight was already filtering through the curtains

and she asked, 'Where is Nathan, and what time is it, John?'

'He's on the phone to the hospital, and it is almost a quarter to eight o'clock.'

'I'd like to go with them, but am not sure if Nathan would rather you were there,' she told him.

'Maybe, but Toby is asking for *you* and that's all that matters.'

'Yes, you're right, of course it is,' she said steadily, and wished that John had felt confident enough to re-assure her with regard to Nathan's desire for her company.

She sat in the back seat of the car next to Toby as Nathan drove them to the hospital. Apart from a brief word of thanks from him for accompanying them, and her telling him that thanks were not necessary in such a situation, they hadn't spoken since they'd left his father's place, but she could feel the depth of his anxiety like a tangible thing.

Taking over the care and wellbeing of a child in Toby's circumstances must be nerve-racking enough without this kind of thing thrown in for good measure, she thought. But apart from that moment of weakness when they'd been hastening to his father's place after he had received the phone call, Nathan was in control again.

Yet she did wish that he didn't feel he had to thank her for being there for the two of them. She'd witnessed his distress when she'd opened the door to him in the early dawn, and seen how much he loved the boy when they'd arrived to find him so poorly. *That* was enough to make her want to be with them every second of the trauma that they were caught up in.

CHAPTER SIX

SHE'D never loved them both so much as at that moment, Libby thought as Nathan drove them to the hospital through the morning rush-hour traffic, the child because he was ill, and the man because he was being cast in the role of the frantic parent.

Holding Toby's hand tightly, she ached to do the same for Nathan, but felt that the memory of what he'd said when leaving her after they'd spent the previous evening together didn't give her the right to do anything other than give him the kind of support that anyone would do in such a situation, which wasn't quite what she had in mind.

Tense behind the wheel, Nathan was aware of how much he needed her, how much she brought stability into his disrupted life, but it wasn't just that, he was in love with Libby. The man who had decided that love was not to be trusted had found that with her it wasn't like that. Life could be so good for them if she would only forgive him.

Since he'd returned to Swallowbrook and got to know her better he'd discovered that it was a passionate, caring woman that he'd once sent away. All his doubts were disappearing as he was getting to know Libby for the person she really was and he wanted her in his life for evermore.

Whether she would believe *that* was doubtful after the way he'd talked about finding himself a wife the night before as if *she* didn't come into it.

When the nightmare they were in the middle of with Toby had been hopefully resolved he would take her somewhere special and propose to her amongst candle-light and flowers. Maybe then she would accept that he was totally sincere in what he had to say.

The months had gone by. Working from dawn to dusk out there, he'd done nothing about the moment of raw awareness that she had awakened in him, until his father had casually mentioned Libby's approaching mar-riage to Jefferson.

It had jolted him into the realisation that he couldn't let it happen without seeing her first, that he had to go back to see for himself if the love she'd had for him was still there. *And much good it had done him,* he thought grimly, with the memory of those desolate moments in the church porch surfacing once more.

He was watching her in the car's rear-view mirror, not-ing how gentle and reassuring she was with Toby, and as the turning for the hospital loomed up ahead the tight band of anxiety across his chest increased its strangle-hold.

When they arrived at Accident and Emergency he carried a drowsy Toby inside, with Libby close by his side. Two of the staff had been alerted by his phone call and were waiting for them, and once they'd been shown into a cubicle a doctor appeared.

'I don't recognise your youngster's symptoms immediately,' he told them when he'd examined Toby, 'and I take it that neither of you are sure or you wouldn't be here. If I had to make a guess I would say that whatever is wrong with him is allergy related, but we don't rely on guesses so we're going to admit him for a couple of days while we do some tests.'

Turning to Libby, he said, 'We have met before, haven't we, Dr Hamilton, at some meeting or other? And this is your family, I take it?'

'I'm afraid not,' she told him with an anxious look at Toby, who was clinging to Nathan and looking really poorly. 'This young patient is Dr Gallagher's ward. We are both employed at the Swallowbrook Medical Practice and live next door to each other.'

'Ah, I see,' he said, and turned his attention to what Nathan was saying.

'One of the reasons we're here is because I'm in the process of adopting Toby,' he explained, 'and have not yet received his medical records from the practice where he and his parents were registered before they were involved in a tragic accident. So I felt that the hospital needed to see him before we began to treat him.'

'Has he eaten anything that could have caused this? Or been near any plant life that could have a sting in its tail?' the other man asked.

'Not that we know of. He spent yesterday with my father and he doesn't let Toby out of his sight.'

'Hmm. So what do the two of you think it might be?' he asked as they bent over the small figure on the bed.

'I thought of urticaria,' Libby told him. 'When he is at his grandfather's place Toby sometimes plays in a field nearby and if nettles are present he could have been stung by them.'

'Yes, but there would have been tears if that was the case and Dad would have picked up on that,' Nathan said sombrely. 'If we are looking at plant life I think that it might be something he has eaten.'

Looking down at Toby, he asked, 'Did you play in the field yesterday?' And got a drowsy nod for an answer.

'And did you eat anything that you found there?'

'Only the grapes,' was the weak reply.

'What kind of grapes were they, Toby?'

'Black and shiny.'

His next question cut into the tension in the room like a knife. 'How many…er, grapes did you eat?'

'Two. I spat the others out because I didn't like them.'

'That's all right, then,' Libby told him gently, and as the three doctors observed each other there was the same thought in their minds. Toby's symptoms could be those of the poisonous plant belladonna, or deadly nightshade, as it was sometimes called due to the serious effects it could have if the berries were eaten.

As Libby stroked his hot little brow gently the doctor took Nathan to one side. 'It does sound as if your young one has been in contact with the so unsuitably named belladonna, or something similar. The vomiting will have brought some of it up, but I'm afraid that we will have to resort to water lavage if blood tests show the belladonna poison is present. Stomach washing out is an unpleasant prospect for anyone, especially a child, but that is what needs to be done immediately if our premonitions are correct.'

The answer they were dreading was there with the test results and the doctor in A and E said, 'Fortunately Toby doesn't seem to have eaten many of the berries, which is a godsend, but the situation is still critical. Hopefully once his stomach has been washed clear of the poison it will prevent any further complications, but it must be done now.'

Nathan nodded bleakly. 'I'm in favour of anything that will save Toby's life so, yes, let's proceed as quickly as possible. Time has been wasted because neither Dr Hamilton or myself had any idea that Toby might have been near belladonna and been tempted by what he thought were black grapes.'

The doctor was already arranging for a theatre to be made available with staff there ready to assist by the time Toby was brought down, and as he was being transferred there, with Libby still holding his hand, Nathan said with his face a grey mask of horror, 'I'm going to insist that I'm there while they do what they have to do. I've done plenty of theatre work while I was abroad, it won't be anything new. But you should get back to the practice, you're needed there more than here. I'll see you when this is over, Libby, and thanks for coming.'

'Will you please stop thanking me? I don't want your thanks,' she told him, stiffening at the abruptness of his dismissal. 'What I *do want* is to know that Toby will soon be well again and that the pain and the nightmare that is there for the parents of any sick child will soon be over for you, and now I'll do what you suggest and go back to my patients, which will leave your father free to come here.'

As Toby's bottom lip began to tremble she said gently, 'I won't be long. I have to go and see to my other sick people now, but I'll bring you something nice when I come back.'

'What will it be, Libby?' he asked with a momentary brightening of his small pale face.

'It will be a surprise,' she told him, and turning to Nathan as the feeling of being no longer needed persisted, 'I would appreciate a phone call when you have a moment to spare.'

'That goes without saying,' he said evenly, and as she went out into the corridor with a heavy heart she didn't hear him groan at the way he'd told her to go as if she'd served her purpose. It *had* been the right thing to do. It was Libby's responsibility as senior partner to be back at the practice, but it had been the wrong way to do it. What was the matter with him? He'd been floundering about like a quivering jelly ever since they'd found Toby in this state, while she'd been like a rock to hold onto, and now he'd sent her away.

They'd arrived at the theatre on the lower ground floor and after that everything else was forgotten as the great machine that was the NHS took over.

The moment Libby arrived back at the practice she was greeted by John, with an extra furrow of worry to add to those that age had carved across his brow.

'So what's the news, Libby? What did they say at the hospital?' he asked.

'It seems as if it might be belladonna poisoning,' she told him. 'When Nathan asked Toby if he'd eaten anything while he was playing in the field, or anywhere else for that matter, he said, yes, he'd eaten some shiny black "grapes", which we think came from a belladonna plant as it describes its berries exactly and his symptoms fit in with what we know of the poisonous effects of it.

'Fortunately he didn't eat many of the berries, just one or two, but he's finding it rather difficult to swallow and is drowsy. Then there's the fact that he has sickness and diarrhoea and his temperature is up, so the doctor in A and E is going to have to wash his stomach out to get rid of any poisonous substance. Nathan is insisting on being there while it is being done so Toby will have him close all the time, thank goodness.'

John was observing her, dumbstruck. 'I was with Toby all the time he was in the field. The only time he was out of my sight was when he was playing at hiding in the bushes and I had to find him, so it would have to be then that he found the berries. I feel dreadful that it should have happened while he was in my care, or that it should have happened at all.'

'You must *not* feel like that,' she told him firmly. 'These things can happen without any blame attached to anyone. How were you to know there was deadly nightshade nearby and that he would mistake the berries for grapes? It is typical of a child to eat what they shouldn't.'

About to set off for the hospital he paused and asked, 'Nathan—how is he coping? These are times when a child needs a mother. I have the feeling that somewhere in the past he took the wrong turning with regard to that. I don't suppose he's ever said anything to you to that effect, has he?'

As if, she thought grimly, and told him, 'No, John, he's never said anything like that to me.'

'I thought not,' he said with a sigh, and drove off to see his adoptive grandson.

There were still a few stragglers in the surgery waiting room and when Libby called the first of them in she was confronted by middle-aged Thomas Miller, leaning heavily on a stick.

He owned the outdoor equipment store in the centre of the village, patronised by many of the walkers and climbers who were attracted to the lakes and fells.

Once a keen climber himself, he was no longer able to enjoy their delights due to a serious leg fracture that he'd sustained while up on the tops. He had been missing for days until the mountain rescue team had found him at the bottom of a gully.

The delay in getting him to hospital for the surgery needed on the injured leg had left him only partly mobile on it, so now he was doing the next best thing to climbing the fells by providing those who still could with everything *they* might need to keep them safe, dry, and fed.

He was a likeable man with a wife and two teenage

sons who had no yearnings to become involved in the sport that had once been their father's favourite pastime.

As well as the store Thomas was chairman of the community centre in the village and almost always had something interesting to pass on when he saw her about what was being planned by his committee.

Before she had time to ask what had brought him to the surgery he was asking for information, rather than giving it, in the form of wanting to know, 'What's wrong with the laddie that Nathan's bringing up, Libby? I've just seen John setting off for the hospital looking very downcast, said he hadn't time to chat as the young'un was very poorly.'

'Yes, he is,' she agreed. 'We had to take him there this morning as we weren't sure what was wrong with Toby. Nathan is there with him now and I've just got back. When something like this happens and the adoptive parent knows nothing about the child's previous medical history it's very worrying.

'Maybe you'd like to pass the word around for the benefit of other children and their parents that it seems as if he has been poisoned by eating the berries of the belladonna plant and at the moment the situation is serious.

'And now what about you, Thomas? What brings you here on this chilly winter morning?'

'I've got a swollen foot on my good leg and thought I'd better come and see you.'

When she'd examined his foot Libby said, 'It looks like an infection of some sort. Have you had a sore or a cut on it recently?'

'I bought some new shoes a few weeks back and they rubbed the skin off one of my toes. It healed up all right, but still felt tender and then the swelling appeared.'

'Hmm, the infection could have originated from that and lain dormant for a while,' she told him as she felt the swollen fleshy part of the top of his foot. 'I'm going to give you a course of amoxicillin. Are you all right with that? You're not allergic to it?'

'No,' he said easily. 'I've had it before without any side effects.' He got up to go. 'Do tell Nathan that I hope the boy will soon be better. We're having a big barbeque on bonfire night on the usual field behind the park and the young'un won't want to miss that.'

'Hopefully we'll all be there,' she told him, with the dread of what Toby had told them heavy on her, and wished that Nathan would phone, but as it was barely an hour since she'd left him maybe she was expecting too much.

She'd been anticipating having to dash around in the lunch hour to find something to take back with her for Toby, but the nurses had forestalled her and one of them turned up at that moment with sweets and toys that they'd collected amongst the staff.

'Is it right that Toby might have been eating the berries of the deadly nightshade?' she asked. 'I heard you telling Dr John something like that and it sounded really awful.'

'Yes,' she told her. 'He only ate a couple, but it is very worrying just the same as the berries can kill.'

At that moment Nathan came through on her desk

phone and the practice nurse departed. 'How's Toby?' she asked urgently.

'Sleeping more naturally,' he replied. 'His tummy should now be washed clear of the poison, and if what they've done at the hospital is sufficient to make him better, we might see some improvement soon. It makes me shudder to think what he would have been like if he'd eaten more than just two of the ghastly things.

'How are things at your end?' he wanted to know. 'Had Dad finished morning surgery when you got back?'

'Yes, more or less. He is on his way to the hospital now. John was devastated when I told him what Toby had been up to and is most upset that it had happened while he was in his care. He said it could only have occurred while they were playing hide and seek in the bushes on the edge of the field. So do please have a kind word for him, Nathan.'

There was silence at the other end of the phone for a moment and then he said dryly, 'Why, what do you think I'm going to do? Blame him for being kind enough to look after Toby during the half-term break?

'I can tell that you're not very pleased with me, Libby, and I apologise for being a tactless fool when I told you to go back to the surgery, but there are others who need you besides Toby. We can't expect to monopolise you all the time. So am I forgiven? I never get it right with you, do I?'

'There is nothing to forgive, just as there is nothing to thank me for,' she told him with a lift to her voice. 'I'll see you this evening as soon as I've finished here.'

When she'd replaced the receiver another patient was waiting to be seen and after that there were twice as many home visits to do because she was the only doctor available. But that was what it was all about and Nathan had been right as usual in insisting that she make the surgery her priority in spite of her longing to be with the two of them.

When she arrived at the hospital in the evening he was sitting beside the bed, watching over Toby, who was sleeping once more with his small chest rising and falling steadily, unlike the distressed breathing of earlier in the day.

But he was still very pale and poorly-looking and as she came to stand beside them Nathan looked up and said with a wry smile, 'He has asked a couple of times when you were coming with the "goodies" so it would seem that Toby's thought processes have not been affected.'

She was bending over the child in the bed, observing him with a glance that was a mix of the keen eye of the medic and the tender concern of someone who cared a lot for the small motherless child and the man watching over him.

It had been a long and tiring day, but it was as nothing compared to what Nathan had been going through, she thought. Yet when she turned to face him the smile was still there, somewhat frayed at the edges but a smile nevertheless. She wasn't to know that just the sight of her after one of the worst days of his life was comforting beyond belief.

However, Libby's thoughts were centred on the urgencies of the moment and she asked, 'So what is the verdict on the gastric lavage and Toby's condition in general?'

'Improving,' he replied soberly. 'The lavage should have washed the poison out of his system and we have to hope that he will gradually recover. Dad has been and gone in an awful state. He's going to investigate all the plant life where Toby was hiding and see it off when he finds the belladonna so that no other child will be tempted to eat what they think are juicy black grapes.

'And what sort of day have you had?' he asked. 'Or shouldn't I ask?'

Nightmarish would be a truthful answer to that question, she thought, with the two of them constantly in her thoughts and a huge workload to cope with.

Instead she told him, 'I've had better, but Hugo will be back tomorrow and then the pressures from the surgery will slacken off, and as for now would you like me to sit with Toby while you have a break?'

'No, Libby. I'll be fine,' he said, not wanting to miss a moment of being with her now that she was there.

He was doing it again, she thought, pushing her away, keeping her on the edge of the trauma he was going through. Was he afraid that she would see their togetherness at this awful time as a bond that might tie him to her?

She wanted to run away and hide, but not before Toby saw that she had kept her promise. Producing the bag of toys and goodies, she said levelly, 'The surgery staff have sent these, everyone is most concerned for Toby and yourself.' And still persisting, she asked, 'Have you had anything to eat since we came here this morning?'

'No. Food would choke me. I've had a few cups of coffee, which are all I've needed so far.'

She nodded and, pulling another chair up at the opposite side of the bed, sat facing him in silence for what seemed like an eternity until Toby opened his eyes and on seeing her asked, 'Have you brought them, Libby?'

'Yes, my darling,' she told him. 'I've brought lots of things for you to eat and play with as soon as you're feeling better. They're in this big bag.' She held it up where he could see it and he nodded then closed his eyes and dozed off again.

Nathan had been silent during their short conversation. As he'd watched the two of them together all his vows to wait until the right moment to open his heart to her had disappeared.

As she was placing the bag in the locker at the side of Toby's bed he rose to his feet and, fixing her with his dark hazel gaze, said in a low voice that she alone could hear, 'Libby, will you marry me? It would be so much the right thing to do.'

'Nathan, how can you ask me that now? Of course I can't,' she breathed, taking a step back on legs that had turned to jelly. 'I'm not in the market for another marriage of convenience, this time yours!' She moved even further away from him. 'I will be here to see Toby this time tomorrow, or before if he needs me, and it would help if you aren't around.'

'You still haven't forgiven me for rejecting you all that time ago, have you?' he said flatly.

'This is not about forgiveness,' she told him in an anguished whisper. 'It's about a word that seems to be missing from your vocabulary where I'm concerned, so subject closed!' And once again she set off down the hospital corridor with pain in her heart.

But this time it was for the *two of them*. It was crystal clear that Nathan's lukewarm proposal had been because he *was* considering her as a mother figure to help him bring Toby up, and this crisis had settled any doubts he might have had. If that was the limit of his affection for her, the miseries of the past would seem as nothing compared to those of the future.

As he'd watched her go he had wanted to chase after her and tell her that his love for her was a clear and constant thing, that since he had got to know her better she was never out of his thoughts. But it was clear from Libby's reaction to his ill-timed proposal that *her* thoughts were not running along the same channels as *his*.

And so what had he done? Let his heart take over his mind and asked her to marry him in the worst possible setting. At a time when she was bound to feel that he wanted her in his life to help with Toby, who was lying beside them recovering from an illness that could easily have killed him, and when all around them was the smell of antiseptic when it should have been lilies or roses.

The only good thing to come out of his crazy impulse was to know that she was still on Toby's case, loving and gentle towards him, *caring for him like a mother*. So if he, Nathan, had put himself beyond the pale in

Libby's estimation, at least her feelings towards Toby weren't going to change.

He loved everything about her, he thought achingly, the golden fairness of her, the soft brown velvet of eyes that were only ever watchful and wary where he was concerned. He admired the way she ran the practice and treated the staff, and sometimes wondered how that father of hers could bear to be so far away from his only child. Yet fool that he was, hadn't *he* stayed away from her for three long years and now was desperate to make up for it?

As Libby drove back to Swallowbrook at the end of one of the most stressful days she'd had in a long time, her spirits were at a low ebb. It had started badly and got steadily worse, the final straw being Nathan's impromptu and emotionless proposal.

Her refusal had been prompt and painful, and she'd had control of the situation until now, but on the last mile of her journey home she was weeping at the futility of her feelings for a man who understood her so little.

Roll on her short vacation in the house on the island in the middle of the lake, she was thinking as she put the car away for the night. Just a couple of weeks and she would be away from everything that hurt.

Hopefully by then Toby would be better, because if he wasn't she wouldn't want to be away from him no matter how desperate she was for some time on her own, and if Nathan was back at the practice along with Hugo she would be able to go away with an easy mind. But for the present the sting of being proposed to because of her usefulness rather than her appeal was not easy to cope with.

Normality was coming back into his life in everything except his relationship with Libby, Nathan reflected on the morning that Toby was discharged from hospital. That had died a death on the day that he'd asked her to marry him and been well and truly put in his place.

It had been crazy to throw away the closeness that had been developing between them in a moment of intense longing, and now there was not a lot left between them, he decided as he drove home with an excited Toby beside him.

She had been diligent in her visits to the boy, and he'd done as she'd asked and kept out of the way in the early evening of each day, which was when she came, using the break from his bedside to go home and have a shower and a change of clothes.

By the time he'd got back she had been and gone. Sometimes they'd passed each other on the way and he'd thought grimly that it wasn't a crime he'd committed. He could think of one or two local, unattached women who would jump at the chance of marrying him, but he didn't want them. He wanted Libby beside him in the dark hours of the night and across from him at the breakfast table. What it was going to be like when he returned to the practice he shuddered to think.

It had been a Friday when he'd brought Toby home from the hospital and he would be going back to school on the Monday. Nathan had seen little of Libby over the weekend, but Toby had spent some time with her as it seemed that she'd promised him on the night before his discharge that he could go across to her place to play whenever he wanted if it was all right with his uncle.

Nathan hadn't had any quarrel with that, just a wish that he might have been included in the invitation, and now it was Monday morning and after seeing Toby safely into school Nathan presented himself at the practice once more with the determination inside him that as far as he was concerned he was there to work, ready to slot himself back into the busy medical centre where at least he would be able to see Libby, even if *she* didn't want to see *him*.

He was in for a surprise. Along with the rest of the staff she greeted him cordially enough, as if nothing between them had changed, and he observed her thoughtfully when she wasn't looking in his direction. He was getting the message. It was going to be business as usual at the surgery and the cold zone at any other time.

It was the first time she had seen him properly in days she was thinking as the morning got under way and noticed that although Nathan was dealing with his patients with his usual brisk efficiency he looked tired and gaunt, like someone carrying a heavy burden, and she felt that her love would be a poor thing if she didn't do something about it, because love him she did, she always had, and no matter what he did or said, nothing was ever going to change that.

CHAPTER SEVEN

AT the end of the morning surgery she said to him, 'Would the two of you like to come for a meal tonight? It would save you cooking as long as you don't mind eating somewhat later than you usually do.'

He was observing her with raised brows but his reply when it came was easy enough. 'That would be very nice, except for the fact that Dad is picking Toby up from school and taking him back to his place for his evening meal to celebrate him being well again. Thanks for the thought, though.'

As she'd listened to what he had to say she knew that the obvious thing to do was to say that the invitation was still open if he wanted to come alone, but she'd been relying on Toby as the bond between them to keep the atmosphere less taut than it had been since Nathan had asked her to marry him as those hurtful moments haunted her constantly.

He was tuned into her thoughts on *this* occasion and said, 'I'm sure you would prefer it if he was with us, so perhaps another time would be better, and by the way, as I don't have to pick Toby up from school, I'm available until we close here if you want an early finish for a change. I can imagine what the workload has been like while Hugo and I have both been absent.'

It was *her* turn to refuse *his* offer. 'I asked you to come for a meal as you look as if you haven't been eating much over recent days, and as this evening will be your first free time since Toby was ill I wouldn't want you to be putting in extra time at the practice on my behalf. So do we understand each other? The offer still stands if you would like to come on your own tonight.'

She wasn't going to tell him that she was achingly aware of the strain he'd been under, and that she could not stop herself from caring about him just as long as he understood that was where it ended. He'd spoiled the rest of it by making her feel that he wanted her as a mother figure for Toby and was seemingly prepared to go along with the *wife* part of it for the child's sake.

He couldn't refuse again, Nathan was thinking. The thought of having Libby to himself for a couple of hours until his father brought Toby home at his bedtime was not to be refused twice, so he said, 'Yes, all right, I'd like that, but before I set off on my house calls I'd like to make it clear that I *will* be working the extra hours this afternoon in spite of what you say.

'I know that you would rather see less of me than more, which makes your invitation to dine with you tonight somewhat of a surprise, but with regard to this place I'm part of a team and am already conscious that my contribution is a lot less than yours, so today I am on full steam.' While she digested that he went out to his car and within seconds drove off to visit the sick in the cottages and in the bigger houses on the leafy lanes that surrounded the village.

Hugo followed him shortly afterwards to do his share of the house calls and while they were gone Libby went across to Lavender Cottage and prepared a casserole, which she put in the oven on a low setting.

Once that was done she laid the table with the cutlery and crockery that had been her mother's pride and joy. Then it was back to the practice where the waiting room was filling up again for the second surgery of the day.

As she crossed the space that separated the cottage from the practice building the lake was glinting in the distance beneath a pale winter sun and the house on the island was caught in its rays as a reminder that soon she would be there, away from the practice for a little while and from the man who was never out of her thoughts.

Maybe when she wasn't seeing Nathan all the time at the surgery and in his comings and goings to the cottage next to hers she might find some peace of mind, if only briefly, she thought, but loving him had become a way of life, a reason for living, even though she was miserable most of the time because of that same love.

At the end of the day they left the building that had once been her home together and separated outside the cottages while Nathan went to change and Libby hurried inside to check that the casserole hadn't dried up.

It hadn't, so she dashed up the stairs, flung off her

working clothes, and after a quick shower put on pale grey slacks and a black silk top and was coming down the stairs when he rang the bell.

Her eyes widened when she saw the bouquet of all the flowers she liked best that he was holding, and as she stepped back to let him in, with her composure slipping into confusion, he handed them to her and said whimsically, 'I'm not going to use the "thanks" word, but I don't know how I would have got through the last couple of weeks without you, Libby. You were my rock to hold onto in the midst of the horror of Toby's illness.'

He was explaining the other side of that ghastly proposal, she thought with tears pricking, and unable to stop herself she reached forward and kissed his cheek.

As he turned his head, surprised by the gesture, their lips met and the moment became a torrent of longing as his arms tightened around her and she gave herself up to kisses that were a much better thing than her lips against his cheek.

The ringing of the doorbell broke into the moment and Nathan groaned as they drew apart. 'Are you expecting someone?' he asked.

She shook her head. 'No, but I'd better see who it is.' Moving towards the door reluctantly, she pulled back the catch to reveal John in the porch, holding a heavy-eyed Toby by the hand.

'Sorry to arrive so soon,' he said apologetically. 'When Nathan rang to say that he would be eating here tonight I told him that I would bring Toby back at half past seven as he'd already been asleep for a couple of hours after school, but his first day back has taken it out of him and he needs to be tucked up in his bed.'

Nathan had appeared behind her. 'It's all right, Dad,' he said, and with a smile for Libby, 'Would you consider bringing the food over to my place while I get Toby settled for the night? It would solve the problem.'

'Yes, of course,' she agreed weakly, still under the spell of his kisses and the joy of being in his arms. There had been none of the awful feeling of being used, just the supreme delight of a moment that had come out of nowhere and might have progressed into something special maybe.

Yet, she thought as John said a brief goodbye and Nathan picked Toby up into his arms ready to take him to where he belonged, some things that happened came in the form of a lesson from life and were meant to cause those involved to stop and think before committing themselves.

As the door closed behind them she took the casserole out of the oven and placed it on a tray, then followed them across, and while Nathan was putting Toby to bed set the table in his dining room instead of hers.

'The sleepy one is asking for a kiss, Libby,' he called down some minutes later. 'Can you come up?' When she appeared in the doorway of the smaller of the cottage's two bedrooms Toby was smiling at her from the pillows and clutching his comforter, which had been with him all the time he'd been in hospital.

As tears pricked she thought how wonderful it would be if she was there every night at his bedtime because Nathan loved her for herself and not her usefulness.

Nathan was watching her expressions change and knew that what his father's ring on the doorbell had interrupted was not going to happen again when Toby was asleep. It had been a moment of bliss that had ended as quickly as it had begun. Once again the timing had been wrong.

His surmise was correct. As they ate the meal that Libby had prepared the conversation was about everything except those kisses, such as their day at the practice and village affairs, including the barbeque and bonfire that was to take place on the coming Friday night.

'There has been that kind of thing on Bonfire Night ever since we were young, hasn't there?' he commented, remembering how she had always been somewhere near on the night. 'That is what is so enchanting about this kind of community. I would imagine that everyone rallied around like they do when you lost Jefferson.'

'Yes, they did,' she said quietly, wishing he hadn't brought up the awful mistake she'd made out of loneliness and rejection while they were in the middle of chatting about general things, and that wasn't the end of it.

'You never talk about your marriage, Libby. Did you love him?' he asked gravely, and more importantly, 'Did he love you?'

He was remembering them again, those ghastly moments in the church porch, and suddenly he had to know if he'd made the second-biggest mistake of his life in thinking that Libby had been totally happy on her wedding day.

'I think I was more in love with love than I was with Ian,' she said, as if the words were being dragged out of her. 'I was in my late twenties with no family around me. I'd lost my mother, and my dad had moved away because he couldn't stand the thought of how he'd had to sell the farm due to his own carelessness.'

There was a pause and he felt himself tense as she continued, 'And you'd made it clear that you had no feelings for me. You never came back. Not even for a visit.

'Ian had already proposed to me twice and I'd turned him down, but the third time…well, you know the rest. With regard to if *he* loved *me*, not in the true sense, I felt. He wanted a wife. I was sitting there on the shelf. In truth it wasn't the marriage I wanted it to be, but the way it ended was a tragedy and not something I'd wish on anyone. It's not something that I like to talk about, Nathan, so can we please change the subject?'

'Yes,' he said with the gravity still upon him, 'but just one thing before we do.'

'And what is that?' she asked tonelessly.

'How in a thousand years could you have ever thought you were on the shelf? Not every guy in Swallowbrook was as blind as I was at that time.'

She shrugged slender shoulders inside the black silk top. 'Maybe they just didn't appeal to me. Ian was different, he didn't ask a lot of me because he was so absorbed in his own lifestyle. I asked him once why he'd married me and he said he'd felt he was at the stage in his life where he should have a wife, and I obviously fitted the bill for him. So you see, neither of our hearts was ever in it. If Ian hadn't died we would have been divorced by now, I'm sure of it.'

They were closer than they'd ever been in these few moments, he was thinking, but Libby wanted to talk about something less revealing and he had promised her that he would, so returning to the subject of Friday night he asked, 'What about the bonfire and barbeque? Have you got something planned, or should the two of us take Toby? Today has exhausted him, it was plain to see, but by Friday he should be more his usual self and if he's not we won't take him. Agreed?'

'Yes,' she told him. 'I haven't made any plans regarding it. I don't have much time, *or inclination*, for socialising these days.'

'So can't we do something about that? When things are really back to normal with Toby, and Dad will have him for the night, why don't we live it up somewhere in the town, or hereabouts if you know of somewhere special?' As she observed him doubtfully he said dryly, 'With no strings attached.'

'Yes, maybe we could do that some time,' she agreed, and thought it wasn't *strings* she was concerned about, it was *bonds*, the bonds of the love that bound her to him, while for all she knew Nathan might be wanting to use her for some light relief in the restricted life that was now his.

She didn't stay long after that. His questions had opened old wounds, brought back the uncertainties of the past that were always there somewhere in the background, and just because the moment they touched they became two different people she wasn't going to turn back into the romantic innocent that had been given her marching orders that day at the airport.

Her timing had been so horribly wrong. There had been weeks before he'd gone when she could have told him how much she loved him, and when he'd casually suggested that she go with him she'd begun to hope.

But in love with him though she was, her loyalties to the practice, his father, her father and to the place she loved most on earth had made her refuse. Hoping all the time that he would change his mind about working abroad if only for a little while, and begin to see her as something other than just a face at the practice.

When she opened the door to leave there was a chill wind blowing and Nathan took a jacket of his off a hook in the hall and wrapped it around her protectively. When she looked up at him from the circle of his arms it was there again, the awareness that was so strong between them. Turning it into trivia before it took hold of them again, she said, 'My door is only yards away. I'm not going to catch cold.'

'Nevertheless,' he said, releasing her from his hold, 'you wouldn't be out in it even for such a short distance if it wasn't for my affairs, and there's no rush to return the jacket. I have others.'

He gave her a gentle push. 'Away with you, and thanks for the food. It would seem that the next time we dine together will be at Friday night's bonfire, subject to Toby not being too tired. Every time I think about what he has recovered from I feel weak with thankfulness.'

'Yes, you must be,' she said gently. 'I was only on the outside of things and I was transfixed with horror, so what it must have been like for you I shudder to think.'

'You helped us to get through it, Toby and I. Without you I would have been in despair. I am so sorry I presumed on your good nature by asking you to marry me, Libby. Obviously we aren't on the same wavelength about that sort of thing and it won't happen again.'

'I would prefer not to talk about that if you don't mind,' she said with sudden coolness, stepping out into the darkness. 'Goodnight.'

He nodded, he'd got the message. After watching her safely cross the distance between their two cottages and close the door behind her, he went in and did the same.

As the week progressed Toby was getting stronger with every day and the three of them going to the bonfire on the Friday evening was becoming a certainty that Libby was looking forward to in one way, but not in another.

She hadn't forgotten the conversation she'd had with Nathan on the Monday night. How he'd wanted to know how much Ian had meant to her. If she'd known that within seconds of her becoming Ian's wife Nathan had rushed through the churchyard and onto a passing bus to get away from the scene he'd just witnessed, she might have understood his questioning better, but as it was she'd found it unnerving.

The morning after the bonfire she was going to the island for the long-awaited break that she'd arranged, and on the Thursday night was intending going into the town to do a big shop as there was no way she wanted to be going backwards and forwards between Greystone House and the village or the privacy she was looking forward to would be gone.

She'd arranged to be taken there and brought back the following Saturday by one of her patients who owned a boatyard on the lakeside and also offered transport on the water to anyone requiring it.

'I'd be obliged if you could take me to the island early Saturday morning before anyone is about,' she'd asked him. Easygoing Peter Nolan, who saw her from time to time for diabetes checks, had said, 'Sure, Libby, I'll take you in the middle of the night if you want, and you can park your car at the yard if you like, so it won't be on view. But are you sure you'll be all right out there on your own?'

'Yes, I'll be fine,' she told him. 'I just want a rest and some privacy.'

'All right,' had been the reply. 'I'll be waiting for you at crack of dawn on Saturday, and by the way the other day I went for my yearly retinol check that the NHS insist we diabetics have.'

'And?' she asked with a smile for the burly boatman.

'The optician said everything was OK behind my eyes and she'll be writing to you with the results.'

'Good. Keep on watching your weight still, won't you, Peter?' she reminded him gently.

Whenever anyone at the surgery asked Libby where she was going for the winter break that she was planning she was evasive and Nathan decided that it was because of him. What did she think he was going to do? he thought sombrely. Ask if he could go with her, like some hungry dog begging for a bone?

After her chilly farewell the other night he felt that their relationship was back at square one again and no way was *he* going to ask what her plans were. Sufficient that they were going to spend Friday evening together with Toby, who was counting the hours.

But a week without her was going to be a long one, though he supposed he shouldn't complain as originally her winter break had been going to be two weeks instead of one.

He didn't know that quixotically she was desperate to be away from him to sort out her thoughts about the two of them. Ever since the night he'd rung her doorbell to ask if she had any milk to spare for Toby's drink Nathan had never been far away.

Yet she also felt that a week would be long enough without seeing him, so she'd reduced her winter break to one week instead of two and saved the other one for Christmas.

He'd seen her arrive home with a big shop from one of the supermarkets on the Thursday evening and decided that wherever she was going it would seem that it was self-catering. When he'd told Toby on the Friday that Libby was going on holiday the following week he'd asked with the uncomplicated mind of a child why they weren't going with her, as to him her presence was now an accepted part of his life.

Toby knew that she loved him just as much as he,

Nathan, did, so he would be unhappy too while she was away. He told him gently that it needed two doctors to look after the people of Swallowbrook, especially in winter time, which meant that he was needed at the surgery while she was away and that was why they weren't going with her.

He wasn't going to explain to Toby that his father was always available in a staffing shortage, and that it was because Libby wanted some time away from himself that she was taking a break. So to take his young mind off her comings and goings he'd drawn his attention to the bonfire, which was no longer in the future. It was glowing and crackling not far away on the field behind the park.

Practically everyone from the village was there in party mood, but not in party clothes. Strong shoes, warm jackets and woolly hats were setting the dress code for the evening.

The members of the event's committee were in charge of the fireworks and Toby's eyes were wide as they exploded in brilliant-coloured cascades in the night sky. Above his head Libby and Nathan exchanged smiles at the extent of his wonderment, and Hugo, who was standing nearby with his sister, said that it was only last year that her two girls had been in a similar state of wonder, but tonight they had promoted themselves to helping with the sale of treacle toffee from a nearby stall.

Their mother was chatting to a neighbour who had appeared beside her and Libby said in a low voice, 'Are things any easier with Patrice? Is she any nearer to accepting Warren's death?'

He sighed. 'Sometimes I think she is and then it all goes haywire again, which makes me wonder if she ever will. She hasn't got your ability to face up to what life hands out to us, Libby.'

She almost laughed. Hugo hadn't been in Swallowbrook long enough to be aware of how she'd married in haste and repented at leisure, and before that had been in love with the man beside her who had come back into her empty, organised life and turned it upside down.

She didn't feel as if she was facing up to anything at the moment and when she turned and met Nathan's dark, inscrutable gaze she wondered what *his* opinion of her was.

Did he think she was a tease who blew hot and cold with him? Or a frigid widow who wasn't going to thaw out just because there were brief moments of sexual chemistry between them?

He wasn't thinking anything of the sort. His thoughts were travelling along different tracks. One of them was the fast line to envy because Libby and Hugo made such an attractive couple, and with the memory surfacing of his inopportune marriage proposal, *also the other guy didn't have a ready-made family, like himself.*

Another track of thought, which was much more basic, was that the smell of the food on the barbeque was making him feel hungry, and when Toby voiced *his* thoughts by asking, 'When are we going to have something to eat, Uncle Nathan?' Libby took the hint and they left Hugo and his sister to carry on doing their own thing.

Unlike previous Bonfire Nights when often rain had sheeted down, the weather was perfect for this one. A winter moon high in the sky was shining down on the scene below, and although the night was chilly, it was warm around the fire and beside the barbeque, and the community spirit that was an essential part of Swallowbrook was giving off a warmth of its own.

As the two doctors and Toby stood amongst the crowd waiting to be served with sausages and beef burgers, followed by parkin and hot drinks, Nathan said, 'It's so good to be back. The work in Africa was hard yet very fulfilling and before Toby came into my life I'd thought I might extend my contract, but everything has changed and it is here that I want to be.'

He was giving her a lead, she thought, an opening to say how she felt about that. If it was what *she* would want him to do, yet he shouldn't need to ask. Did Nathan think she kissed every man who might put his arms around her the way she'd kissed him?

'Growing up in Swallowbrook would certainly be the best thing for Toby,' she told him, keeping it impersonal. 'It was a heavenly place to me when I was young and still is for that matter.'

'I can remember you when you were small,' he said, aware that he'd been sidetracked. 'A chubby little blonde kid with your hair in bunches who always seemed to be tagging along with me and my friends.'

He'd described her exactly, she admitted to herself, and thought how well *she* remembered *him*, dark-eyed, dark-haired, agile leader of the young ones of that time. He used to call her 'pudding' and groan when she appeared.

Years later, when she had joined the practice as a slender, dedicated young doctor with the same golden fairness, her attractions had registered with him, but familiarity had made her seem less appealing than she was because to him she'd still been the kid who'd followed him around like a lap dog all that time ago.

It wasn't until she'd surprised him by turning up at the airport that it had hit him like a sledgehammer with only seconds to spare that he didn't know the woman that she had become as well as he thought he did, and ever since he'd wanted to put that right.

Reminiscing was the last thing Libby had in mind on this cheerful, noisy night beside the bonfire, so she changed the subject and brought the moment back into the present by asking, 'So how do you think Toby is doing now that he's on the mend?'

'He's doing well considering what happened, but it will be a long time before I stop having nightmares about it, and will never cease to be thankful that he ate so few of the berries.'

He would have liked to tell her on a lighter note that he'd kept a promise he'd made to Toby when he'd been in hospital and had bought a boat for the three of them, so that they could sail the lake whenever they chose, but felt that when she heard about it Libby might see it as presuming too much, so bringing his attention back to the bonfire, the fireworks and the food he gave himself up to the pleasure of being there with them both.

The fire had burnt itself out, and all that remained were a few glowing embers.

All the food had been cooked and eaten, and as the three of them walked slowly back to the cottages Nathan said, 'I hope you enjoy your break from the practice, Libby, and also hope that you have given someone details of where you will be staying just in case of any emergencies.'

She shook her head. 'There is no necessity. I won't be far away and will be able to get back quickly if the need arises.'

When they were about to separate she bent and hugged Toby with a feeling that she was making a big thing about a few days on her own. There was nothing to say that she wouldn't be bored out of her mind alone out there on the island, but she needed the respite.

When Nathan had returned to Swallowbrook she had been in a state of joyful amazement. But over recent years she had grown to be wary of life's twists and turns. If there was one thing she didn't want any more, it was heartache.

As he watched her holding Toby close, the feeling that she was eager to get away from him was strong, or else why would she not tell him where she would be for the next seven days?

As she straightened up their eyes met and he said coolly, 'You never used to be so secretive. Is history repeating itself and this time *you* are telling *me* not to wait around?'

It was the first time he'd referred to that since coming back into her life and she replied steadily, 'Not at all. I wouldn't presume to think that I am of such importance.'

On that they separated, with Toby waving sleepily as Nathan unlocked the door and ushered him inside, leaving Libby to step into the quiet of Lavender Cottage with the feeling that their relationship had just taken another backward step.

CHAPTER EIGHT

ALL was still around the lake as Libby drove to the boatyard the next day in the dark of an early autumn morning. She'd loaded her car the night before with all her requirements for the week ahead while Nathan had been occupied in tucking Toby up for the night, and after a quick breakfast had been ready to leave before there had been any signs of life next door.

Now she was wondering if shutting herself away from Nathan for a week was going to make the confusion of her feelings for him any easier to cope with, but the decision was made. When she arrived Peter Nolan was waiting with the motor of his boat spluttering in the quiet morning and once they were off she didn't look back.

When she stepped onto the landing stage at the island and felt the peace of the place wrap around her the doubts disappeared. The boatyard owner observed her dubiously and said, 'Are you sure about this, Libby? It's a bit remote to be out here on your own.'

'Yes, I'll be fine,' she told him confidently, and on that reassurance he began to unload her belongings off the boat and carry them inside while she explored the house.

It was warm and cosy. The fires might be wood-burning stoves not yet lit, but there was also heating and lighting from the house's own generator, which was a pleasant surprise.

She was going to love it here, she thought as she went to watch Peter prepare to set off back across the lake, but still uneasy he said, 'So have I got it right that if folks are curious about where you are, I haven't got to say?'

'Yes,' she assured him, 'you have got it exactly right.'

'So you don't want me to pop across now and then for a cup of tea?' he said jokingly.

'Don't you dare,' she threatened mildly, 'I might be tempted to prescribe castor oil the next time you come to see me if you do.'

When he'd gone she unpacked and then cooked herself a hot breakfast on the top of a magnificent stove to make up for the hasty tea and toast she'd had a couple of hours ago, and her first day at Greystone House began to get under way.

It was daylight now and as she explored the house thoroughly she thought how lovely it was in a cool, un-cluttered sort of way. All the inside walls were painted white, with curtains and carpets dark gold to match modern furniture of relaxing designs.

Around the house was the lake on all sides and though the island was not large it had lots of trees and bushes with walks amongst them. *This is paradise,* she thought, or would be if she knew what lay ahead in her life. She wondered if the property ever came up for sale.

The village school was visible in the distance with the playground empty because it was Saturday. How were Nathan and Toby going to spend their weekend? she thought, and had to remind herself that she had come to the island to have some time away from them, not to be pining, otherwise the whole purpose of her being there would be wasted.

Her relationship with Nathan had moved along then taken a step back a few times since his return and amongst all the other uncertain thoughts that filled her mind was the memory of how he'd commented that if ever he had any children of his own, Toby would be loved just as much as they were. He'd said it with just a hint of regret, as if a family of his own wasn't a certainty for a man who already had a child to bring up.

As darkness fell in the late afternoon and the lanterns came on around the lake, she put down the book she'd been reading and thought she was just as uncertain as he was with regard to whether she would ever have children and experience the joys of motherhood.

For her to do so he, Nathan, would have to be their father and the way they were blowing hot and cold with each other was not going to bring that about, yet she couldn't stop herself from thinking about him no matter how hard she tried not to.

She would have been amazed if she *had* known how he was going to spend his weekend. That after a quiet day for Toby on the Saturday at the end of his first week back at school after the deadly nightshade scare, he had arranged to take him to his father's on the Sunday morning for the rest of the weekend and pick him up from there for school on Monday.

Once he had dropped him off at the lodge by the river he was going to Peter Nolan's place to take possession of the boat, so that when Toby came out of school on Monday afternoon the big surprise would be waiting for him at the moorings at the far end of the lake where privately owned boats were kept.

When he'd purchased the boat and been asked what name he would like painted on it, in a crazily insane moment of euphoria he'd said 'Pudding' and wondered what Libby would think of *that*. Would she understand that it had been chosen in tender humour, or see it as another reminder of how lukewarm had been his interest in her, not just when she'd been small but right up to him going to work abroad?

If she did think that she would be wrong, but she was hardly going to believe that in a matter of seconds at the time of his departure for Africa, he had realised how much she was a part of his life.

On Sunday morning when he went to complete the sale and take the boat out on to the lake, the first thing he saw in the yard was Libby's car parked in front of the office. He observed it in amazement, thinking that his eyes were deceiving him, but the details on the number plate were correct and when he went into the office and asked what Dr. Hamilton's car was doing there, Peter Nolan replied evasively that she'd needed somewhere to leave it while she was away and he'd offered to let her use an empty space on the forecourt.

'But why would she bring it here in the first place?' he persisted as the other man cast a quick glance in the direction of the island.

'Ah,' he breathed as light was beginning to dawn. 'She wanted you to take her somewhere by boat, didn't she, but where?' He looked out onto the lake through the office window. 'Not the island surely!'

The other man nodded reluctantly and said, 'I wasn't happy about leaving Dr. Hamilton there but she insisted she would be fine and it wasn't for me to argue.'

'No, of course not,' he agreed, 'but what is that place like? Is it fit to live in?'

'Absolutely,' was the assurance he was given. 'It is an elegant, away-from-it-all retreat.'

'Hmm,' he murmured doubtfully, and thought he would be getting a close look at it as he sailed the boat past on his way to where he would be keeping it when not in use. Would he be able to resist the temptation to call on the hidden lady of the lake? He doubted it.

Libby and Toby were the two most precious things in his life, the boy because he, Nathan, was the pivot on which his young life revolved, and the woman because of her strength and integrity and the desire she aroused in him. During the last few years he'd come across women who would have been there in an instant if he'd beckoned. But the one that he had on his mind was for most of the time out of reach because of their quixotic past.

As he set sail the sky was dark above and a strong

wind stung his cheeks as the boat ploughed through grey water. The weather was in keeping with the gloom that had settled on him when he'd discovered that it was to the island that Libby had gone in her desire to have some time away from him.

The pleasure of acquiring the boat had been swallowed up by discovering that, but the thought of Toby's delight when he saw it was still there and he was smiling as *Pudding* cut through the water with a comforting chug.

He was nearing the island and straining to see if there was any sign of her. Smoke was rising from the side of the house and as he drew nearer she was there, stoking a bonfire of loose branches and leaves that had been lying around, and he thought grimly that Libby must be desperate for something to do if she was having to do that to pass the time.

The landing stage for the island was close. Risking a rebuff, he began to pull in beside it and was now near enough for her to hear the noise of the motor above the wind.

She turned sharply and as she did so the long skirt she was wearing wafted onto the fire and a tongue of flame curled upwards from the hem.

'You're on fire!' he shouted, and had never moved so quickly in his life. Leaving the motor running, he jumped over the side of the boat onto the stone landing stage and flung himself at her, beating out the flames with his bare hands.

When he was satisfied they were out he looked down

at her sagging in his arms and saw horror and amazement in the eyes looking up into his.

'Where did you come from?' she croaked. 'How did you know I was here?'

'Shall we save that for another time?' he said tersely. 'Right now we need to go inside and treat any burns we might have.' His voice got even tighter. 'What on earth were you doing, having a fire in a gale-force wind?'

She turned her head away and asked in a low voice, 'Where did you get the boat from?'

'It's mine. I've bought it. I picked it up from the boatyard an hour ago.'

'So that's how you knew I was here. Peter told you.'

'Not exactly. I saw your car parked there and wormed it out of him. When Toby ate the poisonous berries and was so ill I promised him I'd buy a boat and tomorrow when I pick him up after school he will see that I've kept my word. He's staying at Dad's place tonight, so I've got some time to myself today.' He looked down at his hands. 'They're beginning to blister where I beat out the flames. What about you, Libby?'

She looked down at the charred fabric of the skirt and said, 'I think you appearing so quickly saved me from anything like that. I'll go upstairs and strip off shortly but first, Nathan, let me look at your hands.' As he spread them out in front of him she saw that he wasn't wrong. The skin was bright red and blisters were appearing.

When she cried out in dismay he said dryly, 'Don't fuss, Libby. Do you have your medical bag with you?'

'Yes,' she replied as the wind howled around them.

'I brought it in case of emergencies, but was not expecting anything of this kind. I'll go and get it.'

He nodded. 'While you're doing that I'll see to things out here before I come inside, such as putting the fire out. I've got a bucket on board and with the lake on your doorstep there's no shortage of water, and then I'll see to the boat, which is reasonably secure as I flung the loop end of the rope over the mooring post as I jumped onto the landing stage. But the motor needs switching off and the rope tightening until I'm ready to leave. It looks as if it's going to be a rough night out there.'

When she came back downstairs carrying the bag he was coming in from outside and looking around him with interest. Pointing to a nearby kitchen chair for him to be seated, she thought that his hands must be really painful, but he sat patiently without a murmur while she put dressings on them that were specially for burns and then brought him a glass of water and painkillers.

'I'm sorry to inflict myself on you like this,' he said when he'd taken the tablets. 'I knew you were here, but wasn't intending calling until I saw you out there stoking the fire. When I saw your skirt was alight I had to do something even though you'd been so secretive about where you were going to spend your break and were so adamant that you wanted to be left alone.

'I was originally on my way to anchoring the boat at the moorings where I'm going to keep it when not in use. It's there that Toby will see it for the first time tomorrow after school, so I will be off shortly and once it is secured will take a taxi back to the cottage.'

'I don't think so,' she said gently. 'Do you honestly

expect that I would let you leave here with dressings on your hands and in pain because of me? You must stay the night and if your hands are no better in the morning I'll fill in for you at the surgery so that Hugo isn't the only doctor there.'

Dark brows were rising as they were apt to do when he had other ideas to what were being suggested. 'I'll accept the offer of a bed for the night,' he said levelly, 'but I've already butted into your holiday once and if you think I'm going to do it again by letting you stand in for me tomorrow at the practice, you're wrong, Libby.

'I'll have an early breakfast, after which I'll moor the boat as I intended doing this afternoon, and then go back to Swallowbrook by taxi. Are we agreed on that?'

'Yes, if you say so,' she said meekly.

He laughed. 'No need to sound so placatory. I'm the one who should be using that sort of tone, having broken into your Greystones idyll. I have to admire your taste, this is a beautiful house.'

'Yes, it is,' she agreed, looking around her. 'It would be fantastic as a weekend home for someone.' *Like us, for instance, if only you would say the 'love' word and convince me that I won't ever have my heart broken again.*

With those words left unspoken she asked, 'How long is it since you've eaten?'

'I had breakfast at seven o'clock.'

'So how about an early lunch?' she suggested, aware that although the quiet she'd been enjoying had been broken into she didn't mind in the least. Nathan was there and she was rejoicing inwardly, not just because he'd saved her from being set on fire but because they would have these precious few hours together that might never happen again.

Looking down at the tattered remnants of her skirt, she said, 'I'll go up and get changed and then we'll have some lunch if that is all right with you.'

'That would be great.'

While they were eating she asked with her glance on the dressings on his hands, 'Do you think we should have gone to the burns unit at the hospital to have your hands treated?'

'Not in this weather,' he said as the wind howled outside. 'I'll see how they are when I get back to the practice in the morning. For the moment the pain is under control. I'll take some more painkillers later before I go to bed,' and with a question in the eyes looking into hers, 'Where will I be sleeping?'

'There are three bedrooms. I've got the big one on the front. There is a ground-floor room just across the hall and a smaller bedroom opposite mine. The one on this level is very attractive. I think you would be most comfortable there.'

I would be 'most' comfortable in yours with you, he wanted to tell her, but didn't know how much of Libby's warmth towards him sprang from gratitude rather than affection because he'd stopped her from getting burnt and been scorched himself in the process.

She may not realise that he wasn't bothered about that as long as *she* was unharmed, but was not going to tell her as the last thing he wanted was to worm himself into her affections by playing the hero. But at least he would have her to himself for a while. *He was inside the fortress.*

After dinner in the early evening they spent the next couple of hours watching a drama on TV and chatting about life in general. Libby brought up the subject of Christmas again and was surprised to find that after her previous mention of it Nathan was well ahead of his shopping for the event, which was more than she was, and rather knocked on the head any ideas she might have had about them doing their Christmas shopping together.

'Would you like to have a look at your room?' she asked when they'd exhausted every topic of conversation they could think of that wasn't about them.

'Yes, sure,' he said easily, and when she'd shown him around he nodded without a great deal of enthusiasm and said with a change of subject, 'I need to check that the boat is safe for the night before I turn in. I won't be a moment, Libby.'

She held out a restraining hand and told him firmly, 'No, I'll see to it. You don't know the layout of the landing stage in the dark like I do.' And before he could protest she'd gone.

The thought of any more harm coming to him was just too much to bear, she thought as she made her way towards where the boat lay still safely tethered. As it rocked to and fro on the surface of the lake a shaft of moonlight brought the name that he had given it into focus and her face stretched.

Painted in black on its dazzling white timbers was the word 'Pudding'.

He had followed her out of the house and as he came up behind her saw that her shoulders were shaking and knew why. *You idiot!* he told himself. *You've upset her. Libby doesn't see it as a joke. Or maybe she does and finds it in bad taste. You aren't going to woo her with that sort of humour.*

She was turning to face him and it was his turn to be taken aback.

It was laughter that her shoulders were shaking with. 'Are you sure you want to call it that?' she gurgled in the dark November night. 'You could run a competition to guess what it means.'

'So you're not mad at me, then?'

Her eyes were wide and luminous in the lights of the landing stage and she said softly, 'Just as long as you don't think I'm a pudding now, how could I be angry with you when you've been hurt because of my carelessness?' Laughter still bubbled. 'I don't think you'll find another boat with a name like that.'

When he took a step towards her she didn't side step or back away. She just stood there and waited for him to take hold of her and when he did it was as if they were on another planet where only they existed as he kissed her until she was limp with longing.

'How am I going to make love to you with hands covered in these things?' he murmured as with arms still entwined they stopped every few moments to kiss on their way back to the house.

'I'm sure you'll find a way,' she breathed with all her

doubts and uncertainties disappearing as the wonder of the night closed in on them.

When they were inside he pointed to the downstairs bedroom and said, 'Do I *have* to sleep in there, Libby?'

'Not unless you have powers that I am not aware of and are going to make love to me by remote control,' she said softly, and taking his hand led him towards the stairs.

It was how she'd always known it would be if they ever got that far, she thought as they made love. The wasted years were forgotten, the future was beckoning, and when at last she slept in his arms it was with the knowledge of just how much Nathan loved her.

Until she awoke the next morning to find him gone, and a note on the pillow beside her that turned a grey November day into a black hole. It said,

> *Libby,*
> *Am ashamed that that I took advantage of your gratitude with regard to the incident with the fire, and those brief but memorable moments when you saw your childhood name on the boat.*
> *I had invaded the privacy that you were so desperate for and then proceeded to use it to my advantage. At the time that I was doing so it seemed the right thing to do, but when I awoke in the dawn and found you curled up beside me I wasn't so sure. None of what happened was how I'd planned it was going to be since I came back*

*to Swallowbrook. I do hope you will understand
that and we can still be friends.*

   *Be careful on your own out here and don't light
any more fires,*

   Nathan.

When she'd read the note Libby sank back against
the pillows, too stunned for tears. Surely Nathan wasn't
saying that the night before had been just a one-off that
he'd engineered because he'd known she was vulnerable and willing due to what had happened previously,
and now he'd gone, leaving a note instead of telling her
to her face that he was still not willing to commit himself?

   Fair enough, he wanted them still to be friends, did
he, so friends they would be when Toby was around and
at the practice, but for the rest of the time he would not
exist as far as she was concerned. He'd made her feel
cheap and cheap she was not!

Nathan had left the island at six o'clock with the motor
of the boat not at full throttle so as not to awaken her,
but once he was clear of the place he sailed at full
speed and once the boat had been moored did as he'd
said he would do, took a taxi back to his cottage in
Swallowbrook where he showered and changed before
picking Toby up for school and then on to the practice.

   Everything was going to plan at this end, he thought
as he ate a hasty breakfast, but what about Libby on the
island? She would have read his note by now and he
prayed that she understood what he'd meant by it.

He'd wanted her so much and when she'd responded to him the night before like she had he'd taken the moment, made love to her and it had been fantastic. But afterwards he'd wished that he hadn't got carried away and had waited as he'd planned to do until he knew that she was sure of him, trusted him not to break her heart again, and now he was thinking that by leaving her the note he might have done that all over again.

Toby was full of what he and Grandfather Gallagher had been doing by the riverside when he called at his father's place to take him to school and John, who knew about the surprise he was planning for him, said when he wasn't within hearing distance, 'You look a bit down. Did you get the boat?'

'Yes,' he replied, forcing a smile. 'I'm taking him to see it this afternoon after school. Do you want to come?'

'No,' was the reply. 'Let it be just the two of you there when he sees it for the first time. I'm going to put my feet up for the rest of the day. Your boy takes a bit of keeping up with, but I wouldn't want to miss having him here for the world. He's given me a new reason for living, and for Toby you're giving him everything you can to make him happy except maybe a woman in his life, a mother figure.'

'Yes, well, they don't sell them down at the supermarket, you know.'

'Which is perhaps all to the good,' his father commented dryly. 'He talks about Libby a lot. Is there anything that he and I can look forward to in that direction?'

'There might have been once,' he said flatly, 'but I made a mess of things and she is wary of me now, so don't raise your hopes only to have them dashed. Maybe Santa might have a mummy for Toby when he comes.'

'Now you're being flip about something very important,' he was told, and Nathan thought that his approach to Libby was anything but flip. If it was he would already be making capital out of the happenings of the night before instead of taking a step back to give her time to take a long look at what had happened in the house on the island.

As if to give emphasis to the conversation he'd just had with his father, Toby asked on the way to school, 'Will Libby be there when I get home this afternoon?'

'I don't think so,' he said gently, 'but I've got something to show you that I think you will like.'

'What is it?' he wanted to know.

'It's a surprise.' And as the school gates were looming up ahead Toby had to be satisfied with that.

When Nathan arrived at the practice Hugo asked in surprise, 'What's wrong with your hands?'

'I had an argument with a bonfire,' he said with a dismissive shrug of the shoulders, and then had another question to answer when the other man said, 'I don't suppose you've heard from Libby at all, have you?'

He sighed. For some reason she was the main topic of conversation this morning when all he wanted was to be left alone to gather his thoughts, which had been almost impossible since he'd left the island at half past six to anchor the boat, then gone home to change, and finally had driven to the lodge by the river to pick Toby up.

But Hugo was asking out of genuine concern and, knowing that Libby would not want her whereabouts to be public knowledge after the way he'd gatecrashed her quiet time and turned it into a night that she would either want to remember always or be in a hurry to forget, he said, 'No, nothing as yet, Hugo, but she has only been gone a couple of days.' And then steered the conversation towards practice matters.

The two of them had decided that today Hugo would do the house calls, while Nathan took Libby's place, with one of the nurses to assist, at the Monday morning antenatal clinic. When she had dealt with blood-pressure checks and sent off any urine or blood samples that were required he would see each one in turn to make sure that the pregnancy was progressing satisfactorily and he found that even there Libby's name was cropping up.

'Where is Dr. Hamilton today?' one of them asked. 'It's unusual for her not to be here.'

'She's taking a short break,' he said levelly, 'and will be with you as usual next week.'

Most of them were in good health and giving no cause for alarm, but when the nurse informed him of the results of the blood-pressure reading for one of them, he told an apprehensive forty-year-old who was expecting her first child, 'I'm afraid we're going to have to give you some bed rest as your blood pressure is very high. I'm going to send for an ambulance to take you straight to hospital because you need to be under their immedi-

ate supervision.' As the colour drained from her face
he told her reassuringly, 'It can happen to any pregnant
woman that their blood pressure gets out of hand. Once
you are resting it should level out and it will be moni-
tored constantly all the time you're there.'

'It's our first baby,' she told him, dabbing at her eyes.
'We've waited so long for me to become pregnant, we
couldn't bear to lose it.'

'Of course not,' he sympathised. 'That's why I've
sent for an ambulance. While you are waiting, have a
word with the receptionist if you want your husband to
be contacted, or anyone else that needs to know what
is happening.'

When the ambulance had been and gone and the
clinic was over it was back to seeing his own patients
and the first ones to present themselves were a young
mother with a little girl of a similar age to Toby.

'So what is the problem?' he asked with a smile
for the child when they'd seated themselves opposite.
He'd seen her following Toby around in the school
playground like a small golden-haired shadow and had
thought it was like history repeating itself.

'Cordelia has got a sore eye,' her mother said. 'She
was poked in it by one of the boys in her class yesterday. I bathed it when we got home but it doesn't seem
to have had much effect. When she woke up this morning it was all red and sticky around the bottom lid.'

'Can I have a look at your eye, Cordelia?' he asked
gently, and she nodded solemnly. It was as her mother
had said, quite inflamed, and when he'd finished checking that the eyeball wasn't damaged and that the sore-

ness was reserved for the membranes of the socket he told her mother, 'I'll give you some drops that should clear it up in a day or two, and if you still aren't happy when you've used them all, come back to see me again.'

As they were about to go he said to the child, 'It wasn't Toby who poked your eye, was it, Cordelia?'

She shook her head emphatically and her blonde ponytail swung from side to side with the movement as she told him still in solemn mood, 'No. Toby is my friend.'

Her mother butted in at that moment to say, 'Everyone thinks you're doing a wonderful job with the boy, Dr Gallagher. It can't have been easy.'

He didn't reply, just nodded, and as they departed he considered that compared to sorting out his love life, caring for Toby *was* easy.

CHAPTER NINE

WHEN they arrived at the moorings in the late afternoon it was a much better day than the one before. The wind had dropped and a pale sun was shining down onto the assortment of craft there. When Nathan pointed out the boat that was theirs, Toby's delight and excitement was a pleasure to behold and would only have been made more gratifying had Libby been there to share it with him.

Before he took Toby on board he fastened him into the life jacket that he'd bought from the Outdoor Pursuits store. Nathan knew he could swim, his parents had seen to that, but he was taking no chances as they pulled out onto the lake.

This time he didn't go anywhere near the island. It would soon be dark and he didn't want Toby to have any diversions on his first sail on *Pudding*. That was what he was telling himself anyway and it was true in part. The last thing he wanted was for the child to be involved in the complexities of his relationship with Libby while on his maiden voyage, but it was an effort not to keep casting his eyes across to where the island stood remote and still on the autumn afternoon.

* * *

If Nathan's day had been full, Libby's had been an aching, empty void. She'd thought the night before that it was all coming right between them at last until he had done what he always did, pushed her away again with just a few words on a scrap of paper. Thank goodness she was here on the island away from everyone, she thought as she gazed out onto the lake's now calm waters. She needed this time alone more than ever.

It was her third day at Greystone House, and she had the rest of the week to concentrate on putting up her defences once more. She'd done it before often enough and would do it again when next the two of them met, she decided determinedly, so why was she weeping all the time and in the late afternoon straining for a sight of Nathan as he took Toby out in the boat for the first time?

She knew what his plans for the day were, and it went without saying that he would be taking the excited five-year-old for a sail about that time, but there was no sighting of them and she went back into the house knowing he wasn't going to be coming calling again unless she asked him to—*and she was not going to do that!*

It was Saturday morning and she was packed and ready to depart, leaving the house as she'd found it, a place to dream in, but not, it seemed, for her.

Peter was due any moment to take her back to Swallowbrook, back to the bosom of a busy practice, back to a relationship that was more of an endurance test than anything else since Nathan had come back into her life. She couldn't believe that he'd thought she'd let him make love to her out of gratitude, or because of their brief rapport when she'd laughed at the name he'd chosen for the boat.

Yet she had to admire him for one thing. Most men would accept what had happened between them without giving a second thought to the whys and wherefores of it, but not so Nathan Gallagher. What he'd said in the note he'd left had hinted that the night they'd spent together had been a mistake and it had besmirched the memory of it, made it seem cheap and fortuitous. She could not forgive him for *that*.

When Peter arrived his first words were in the form of an apology for letting Dr Gallagher find out where she was. 'He guessed when he saw your car parked at my place,' he told her awkwardly, 'and I couldn't deny it. I hope it didn't cause any problems, Libby.'

'No, not at all,' she assured him. There was no way she was going to let Peter be dragged into their affairs, neither was she going to tell him what it was all about. The folks in Swallowbrook had already watched her make one mistake by marrying Ian and, as they always were for their own, had been there for her every step of the way.

It would grieve them beyond telling if they had to watch her make another mistake. It did at least seem as if Nathan's hasty departure from the island and 'the note' had saved her from doing that.

The cottage when she got back was how she'd left it, attractively furnished, tidy and soulless. There were no signs of life next door but as it was Saturday morning she wasn't surprised. Nathan would either have gone into the town to shop or taken Toby to the park, she decided, and if that was so she would have a few more hours' grace before their next meeting.

She was wrong on both suppositions. When she went to the local store to shop for fresh food to replenish her stock after being away, Libby could hear music, and when she turned the corner to where the village hall stood back beside the shops, the fact that Christmas was only a few weeks away was brought to her notice with a jolt.

Morris dancers, dressed in bright colours with bells jangling in the crisp morning, were performing on the forecourt of the hall, and behind them was the Christmas market that the shops and stall-holders held at this time of year.

When she stopped to watch them she saw Nathan and Toby in the crowd on the opposite side of the road and was about to turn away when it seemed that she'd been seen. She heard Toby shout, 'There's Libby!' When she looked up the two of them were coming towards her, with Toby beaming his delight and Nathan observing her gravely.

The urge to depart with all speed was strong, but Toby was not to blame for her fixation for his guardian. He was straining to get to her through the crowd and when they stood in front of her she swept him into her arms and hugged him.

'So how is my beautiful boy?' she asked laughingly, as if she hadn't a care in the world. 'What have you been up to while I've been away?'

'That's what I want to tell you,' he said excitedly. 'We've got a boat, Libby!'

'Wow! When did this happen?' she asked, looking suitably surprised.

'Monday after school,' Nathan said as if she didn't know.

'And guess what it's called?' Toby cried.

'I'm sure I have no idea. What *is* it called?' she asked, as if it wasn't imprinted on her mind for ever. She'd laughed when she'd first seen it, but now she felt it was another reminder of how Nathan still saw her as someone on the edge of his life, rather than at the forefront of it.

'It's called *Pudding*,' he said, unaware of its origin, and turned to Nathan. 'Can Libby come with us the next time we go sailing?'

'Yes, of course,' was the reply, 'if she wants to, that is. How about tomorrow morning?' he suggested promptly, not wanting her to go and knowing that Toby would give him no peace until she'd sailed on it with them.

'I could never say no to Toby,' she told him. 'I've got a life jacket somewhere.'

Libby would be so good to be around him while Toby was growing up, Nathan thought. She was just what the child needed to fill the empty place in his young life. He knew how much she loved him, but would she want himself as part of the package? That was the question. From the frost in her voice when she wasn't speaking to Toby it was almost certain that the answer to *that* would be no.

She'd made it quite clear that night at the hospital when he'd asked her to marry him that she was not in the market for a marriage of convenience and what he was thinking now was that kind of thing.

She would always love the child devotedly, but not the man. Unless he could convince her that the caution he displayed in his approach to her was because of the past flippancy he'd shown for her love for him and the careless words that he'd dismissed it with.

Added to that was always the thought that she would never have married Jefferson if he, Nathan, had not been so blinkered. But maybe he'd been playing it *too* cool, that he'd been patient long enough and was hurting her once again in the process.

He was by nature a man of action, not a ditherer, and as he brought his thoughts back to where Libby and Toby were chattering away, happy to be together again, he felt that his cautious approach had gone on long enough.

On observing that he was back from wherever his mind had been during the last few moments, she said, 'I'm afraid that I have to go. I'm here to do some food shopping as my larder is bare. I'll see you both in the morning, but before I go, Nathan, what about your hand, how is it now? Did the dressing prevent the blistering and take the soreness away? I've been wondering all week if you had to go to A and E.'

'My hand is fine.' He was holding it out in front of him for her to inspect and commented dryly, 'You could have phoned.'

'So could you,' she parried. 'Yet maybe it was as

well that neither of us did. We might have said things
that we regretted afterwards.'

'Such as?'

Toby was engrossed in what was going on around
him at that moment and she said in a low voice, 'Such
as how could you liken the first time we'd ever made
love to a vote of thanks on my part and an opportunity
not to be missed on yours?'

He was not to be ruffled, was actually smiling, and
she thought despondently that he didn't care. Nathan
didn't care what he did to hurt her, and with a brief word
of farewell and a kiss for an innocent Toby she left them
and went to shop.

She drove into the town to do some Christmas shopping in the afternoon after watching the morris dancers
and buying food from the stalls of the Christmas market in the morning, and after a quick lunch in a bistro
went to choose gifts for Toby, John, her father far away
in Somerset and the practice staff, and then there was
Nathan. It would be the first time she had bought him
anything on her own and it wouldn't be easy.

When he'd been part of the practice before she'd
contributed as a junior doctor to the gifts that the staff
bought for the partners, which had been an impersonal
sort of arrangement, but now there was nothing impersonal in their dealings with each other, far from it,
but neither was it a situation for bestowing on him the
kind of gifts she'd always wanted to buy, so how was
she going to get around that? Certainly not a voucher

from one of the big stores, their relationship wasn't so cut down to size as that.

For Toby, whatever she chose she would have to consult Nathan, first, to make sure that he hadn't got the toy already and, second, to check that Nathan hadn't bought it for him as part of the delights of Christmas morning.

It had been a phone call she'd been reluctant to make, but it would be easier than speaking face to face, she'd decided, and when his voice had come over the line it was almost as if the rift in their relationship hadn't happened. When they'd discussed what Toby would like at length he'd said casually, 'And what would you like for Christmas, Libby?'

That had brought the conversation back down to basics and her reply had even more as she'd told him, 'Just peace of mind would be fine.' And before he'd been able to pursue that line of reasoning, she'd rung off.

He hoped to present her with more than that, he thought in the silence that followed, and was already taking steps in that direction. Asking her out to dinner was going to be the first. He'd once suggested that they go out somewhere if his father would have Toby for the night, so the idea wasn't going to come as a complete surprise when he came up with it, but whether Libby was still in the same frame of mind as she'd been then remained to be seen.

When he saw her return in the late afternoon he went out to ask her, and as she faced him with the car behind her full of packages he said, 'Do you remember we once discussed going out on the town if Dad would have Toby for the night?'

'Yes,' was the reply. As if she could ever forget anything he'd said, though it might be better if she could.

'So what do you think? Would you like me to take you for a meal to somewhere of your choice? I've already squared it with Dad that he'll have Toby.'

'Yes, I suppose so,' she told him, hating herself for being so easily swayed. 'If that's all you're suggesting, I suppose we could. As we said at the time, neither of us has much opportunity for socialising so it would be a change, but as far as I'm concerned that is all it will be, a nice meal in pleasant surroundings.'

'Sure,' he agreed, 'but it would be a treat if you wore the blue dress.'

'Why, what for?'

'Because it suits you maybe.'

'I'll think about it, but don't be surprised if I don't.'

There was still frost about, he thought, and as if unaware of it asked, 'So where do you want to go and when?'

'My favourite place is on a wide ledge high up on one of the fells. It's called the Plateau Hotel,' she replied, 'and if we're going there I think it should be soon as it gets booked up very quickly at this time of year.'

'So what about tomorrow night, sailing on the lake in *Pudding* in the morning and dining at the Plateau in the evening?'

'Er, yes, I suppose so,' she said, taken aback at the speed with which he was ready to act on her suggestion.

'So that's sorted, then,' he replied, and again she de-

spised herself for being so amenable after recent events
having been so hurtful.

He was eyeing the car and asked, 'Can I give you a
hand with your shopping?'

She shook her head. 'No, I can manage, thanks just
the same.'

He didn't persist. 'All right, I'll go and see what Toby
is up to, then.' And off he went to get in touch with the
restaurant.

A phone call while she was sorting out her purchases
of the afternoon was to say that he'd made the reser-
vation for eight o'clock the following evening, which
would give them time to drop Toby off at his father's
place and drive up to the high plateau from which the
hotel had got its name.

Back in her own bed that night Libby was finding sleep
hard to come by. She'd agreed to go sailing on the lake
with Nathan and Toby the next morning and how awkward was that going to be? she kept thinking. The three
of them in close proximity with Toby happy and excited
because she was there, and Nathan playing it cool as he
always did, *except for that night on the island.*

And now to add to her sleeplessness even more, she'd
agreed to dine with him in the evening and could see
that being another nerve-stretching occasion.

Sailing the lake the next morning in the smart new
boat was Toby's special time, she thought, and put her
anxieties to one side as the two of them smiled at his
excitement.

Living near the lake, they'd both been brought up amongst sailing craft and it was like history repeating itself from the days when they'd been young and *their* parents had smiled at *their* excitement on the occasions when they'd been on the water in *their* boats.

They stopped for lunch at one of the restaurants beside the water and as Libby looked at his young face glowing from the nip of the wind she hoped that if Toby's parents, taken from him so tragically, were anywhere nearby in the ether, they would be content to know that he was being loved and cherished by the two of them.

If her relationship with Nathan could be as strong and sure as the one they both had with Toby, life would be so wonderful, she thought wistfully, and hoped that she wasn't inviting more uncertainties on herself by accepting his invitation to dine with him that evening. *And it wasn't going to be in the blue dress.* It belonged to a better understanding between them than the present one.

Dressed in warm trousers and sweaters, and with wind cheaters beneath their life jackets, the three of them spent another hour on the lake when they'd had lunch and at one point the house on the island came into view.

Libby was conscious of Nathan's glance on her as the memory of what had happened between them there on a magical night came back, and she turned away. As always at the end of that mind picture was the moment when the putdown had occurred the following morning.

She was tempted to tell him that the dining-out arrangement was off. If his sombre expression was anything to go by, he was reading her mind and didn't need telling, but she told herself there was no cause to make a big drama out of going for a meal with him—that was all that it would be, for heaven's sake. She intended to make sure of *that*.

When they'd left the boat behind and driven back to the cottages Nathan said levelly, 'So are we still on for tonight?'

She was bending to give Toby a hug and looked up at him with an expression that was giving nothing away. 'Yes, I thought we had agreed…hadn't we?'

He was smiling. 'Just checking, that's all.'

As the afternoon wore on she was restless and on edge. Why had she agreed to this evening's arrangement? she kept asking herself. It was bound to be an ordeal, making polite conversation with Nathan when the only words she wanted to hear from his mouth were 'I love you'. If it wasn't for Toby she would steer clear of him altogether, and doing that would not be easy.

Working at the surgery with him, living next door to him, what chance would there be of that? There *was* a solution, of course—leave Swallowbrook, go elsewhere to practise medicine and start a new life. But to do that she would have nothing left of the things dearest to her and that would be worse than what was happening now.

On impulse she put on the warm jacket and the hat she'd worn for the sail on the lake and went out into the village to try to banish the blues.

There was hammering coming from the square in the

centre where the war memorial was situated, and next to it council workmen were erecting the big Christmas spruce that they brought every year to be a focal point in the village.

In the fading light she saw that fairy lights were already beginning to appear in cottage windows and on trees in the gardens. Inside the grey stone properties were her patients and her friends, and next door to her was a man who held her heart in his careless hands, always had, always would.

If it wasn't for it being Toby's first Christmas in Swallowbrook and the first one since he'd been orphaned, she would go away for the two days that were all they allowed themselves at the practice, and that would be a first, absent from the village at Christmas. But if she was filling one of the gaps in Toby's life to some small degree, she had to be there for *him*.

The vicar and his family were arriving home from a drive out in the already frost-covered countryside and as she was passing the vicarage they invited her in for a hot toddy.

As they chatted, the man who loved Swallowbrook almost as much as she did was reminded that so far there were no Christmas weddings arranged to take place in the village this year, which was unusual, and with his glance on Libby hoped that one day, whatever the season, he might have the pleasure of officiating for the caring young doctor who had her own special niche in the life of the place.

Surrounded by the warmth of the vicarage family's welcome and the hot drink they'd provided, Libby's spirits were lifting and as dusk became the darkness of night she made her way home with a lighter step than when she'd set out.

Yet it didn't stop her from remembering how what she'd thought had been the beginning of bliss had turned out to be a raw and aching memory of a non-event that Nathan had felt warranted an apology, and now she was committed to an evening of polite conversation and strained smiles.

Before she went up to change she wrapped the Christmas gifts she had bought for Nathan and Toby, a cashmere sweater for the man and for the boy a battery-operated replica of the boat called *Pudding* that he would be able to sail in the bath. There hadn't been any need to consult Nathan again as to what she should get him. Once she'd seen it in one of the toy shops her mind had been made up.

As she'd been about to wrap the sweater she'd held it close for a moment and wished that Nathan was inside it, that she could hold him close and tell him how much she loved him, but the road of rebuff was a painful one to travel, and she'd been down it too many times.

For her father she'd bought a smart towelling robe and as she wrapped it wished she saw more of him, but he seemed contented enough where he was, so there was no point in fretting.

A camera was her gift for John, who had a special place in her heart, and now all that she still had to shop for were gifts for the practice staff.

Christmas was only a month away and what it would bring with it she didn't know, but had a dismal feeling that Santa wouldn't have any nice surprises for *her* in his sack.

Yet she wasn't quite right about that. The thought had no sooner entered her head than the phone rang, and as if by wrapping his gift she had conjured him up, her father's voice came over the line and it was more buoyant than it had been for a long time.

As he explained the reason for his call his upbeat tone was easily understood. It seemed that he was coming to Swallowbrook for Christmas and bringing someone with him, the new woman in his life. They would be staying with John at his invitation and he hoped she would be happy for him when she met Janice. 'It doesn't mean that I've forgotten your mother, you know,' he said awkwardly. 'I've been like a lost soul since she went.'

'Yes, I know you have,' she told him reassuringly, 'and, Dad, of course I'm happy for you.'

When they'd finished the call she put the phone down slowly. She'd meant what she'd said to him, but couldn't help feeling that she really was going to be the odd one out during the festivities.

But there was no time to mope. The clock said that it was time to start preparing for the evening ahead and the final result was far from what she would have chosen if she'd been looking forward to it.

She'd decided to wear a starkly simple black dress that fitted her mood, relieved only by a gold necklace and matching earrings, and on observing herself in the mirror thought that it went well with the pale face looking back at her and the lacklustre expression.

One thing was clear, she decided, after tonight

Nathan wouldn't be falling over himself to wine and dine her again after her performance of death's head at the feast.

They had taken Toby to the lodge by the river, complete with 'comforter' and his favourite teddy bear, and now Nathan was pointing the car in the direction of the hotel on the plateau beneath the tops of the fells.

He had made no comment about the absence of the blue dress, had just observed her thoughtfully when he'd answered her knock on the door of his cottage and suggested that she get in the car as he and Toby were ready so they might as well get mobile.

Of the two of them he was the most distinguished-looking in a smart grey suit with matching shirt and tie. Where Libby had felt she was underdressed for the occasion she thought that his clothes were a bit over the top for a casual night out, but could not deny that his appearance was heart-stopping, with regard to *her* heart anyway.

Since they'd kissed Toby goodnight and taken the road out of the village there had been no conversation between them and now Nathan's only comment was, 'There is snow on the tops and the forecast isn't good. Gale-force winds and sleeting rain are moving in and if it turns to snow at this level it will be tricky.'

'So do you want to turn back?' she asked quickly.

'No. I'm used to this road,' he said levelly. 'I won't let you come to any harm.'

She almost groaned out loud. Some night out this was going to be, with ghastly weather blowing in and

Nathan as chatty as one of the large stones that in a by-gone age had been strewn along the side of the road by the elements. She wasn't to know that his insides were clenching at the thought of what he would do if tonight, which he'd had such hopes for, turned out to be a fiasco in the storm-lashed hotel that Libby had chosen. Not so long ago he'd decided that he was being too wary of the past in his dealings with her and a more forthright attitude was called for, so he'd suggested that he take her out to dine with a view to clearing the air between them once and for all, and the earth would have to open up and swallow the Plateau Hotel before he would be willing to turn back.

Their table was ready and as they looked around them it was clear that the weather had made others think twice about dining there on such a night, and they had either cancelled or not been willing to make the effort without a booking in such weather.

Nathan's smile was wry. He'd wanted to have her to himself this evening and he'd got it, but it wasn't exactly as he'd hoped it would be as they ate in silence in the empty restaurant, and when they were seated in the hotel lounge with coffee and petit fours amongst a scattering of people who had just stopped by for a drink to take away the chill of the winter night, there was still no rapport between them.

This was catastrophic, Libby was thinking. She should have followed her instincts and refused the invitation to dine with Nathan, yet it would soon be over, it would have to be. Neither of them would want to be stranded up here with nothing to say to each other in this ghastly weather. As soon as they'd finished their coffee they needed to be off.

A gust of cold air in the reception area close by and the loud voices of new arrivals broke into her thought processes and almost simultaneously two men dressed in mountain rescue gear appeared in the doorway of the lounge.

'I know these guys,' Nathan said. 'I used to be part of their team before I went to work abroad. What are they here for, I wonder?' Rising from his seat, he went across to speak to them.

'We're looking for a volunteer to go up to the tops with us as we're short on members tonight,' one of them told him. 'Two teenagers are missing from a group who are staying at the youth hostel on the bottom road. Should have been back hours ago. Their friends reckon they aren't experienced or well equipped, so fast action is needed. How are you fixed for joining us, Nathan? We might need a doctor if we find them.'

'Yes, all right,' he agreed soberly. 'But as you can see I'm with Libby Hamilton from the surgery in Swallowbrook, I need to explain what is happening… And what about equipment? I can't go dressed like this.'

'The hotel has a stock of clothes for this kind of situation. We'll sort that out while you make your apologies to Dr Hamilton.'

'What's wrong, Nathan?' she asked anxiously when he came back to her side.

'Two youngsters lost on the tops,' he said grimly. 'They want me to go with them, Libby. I hope you'll forgive me for leaving you like this but, whatever you do, don't set off homeward bound, will you? I'll come straight back for you once we've found the teens.'

She was observing him aghast. 'I'd rather be up there with you,' she protested.

'No way. I want you here out of the cold, waiting for me, when I return.'

'You're risking your life up there. Suppose you don't come back?'

'I *will* come back,' he said steadily, 'because I have so many things to say to you that I've left unsaid, and then there's Toby, who needs us both so much. I know the fells as well as anyone and I'm trained for this sort of emergency. There's no way I can leave two kids stranded any more than you could. I have to do this, Libby.'

The manager of the hotel was approaching with the necessary equipment that he would need and minutes later he was gone in the company of the two mountain rescue team members with a long backward look in her direction.

CHAPTER TEN

WHEN the three of them had opened the door to go out into the night the wind had been howling even more and, crouched by the fire in the lounge, Libby prayed that it would stop.

Over the years high gusts had been known to blow the unsuspecting off ledges to almost certain death in rock-strewn gullies below, and she thought there would be parents somewhere, frantic to think that their young ones had been caught out by the weather and their own inexperience.

Or it might be that the folks in question didn't yet know that there was a problem and had that frightening moment yet to come.

A hush had fallen over the room with their departure and as she stared blindly into space all she could think of was how the evening that had been so empty and unsatisfying had become a time of praying for the safe return of the victims and their rescuers.

Supposing Nathan didn't come back, she kept thinking, and she'd never told him how much she really did love him? The future would be a black hole if she never saw him again.

The hotel staff were keeping her supplied with hot drinks and as the hours crept by, as if in answer to her prayers, the wind was lessening and the snow that had threatened earlier hadn't yet fallen, but it didn't give any indication to those waiting below what it might be like higher up.

They had no way of knowing what was happening until the door burst open and the two mountain rescue men appeared, carrying a lightweight stretcher with a teenage girl on it wrapped in blankets.

They were followed by a youth of a similar age who was also draped in a blanket, and Nathan was bringing up the rear.

When she saw him Libby's heart leapt with thankfulness. He held out his arms. She ran into the safe circle of them like a homing bird and as he looked down at her their love for each other was there, strong and sure.

'Are you all right?' he asked in a low voice.

'I am now,' she told him joyfully as her life righted itself, 'but I wasn't before. I kept thinking what it would be like if we never saw each other again after wasting so much time.'

'Me too,' he said sombrely. 'As I took one long look at you before I walked out of the door with those two guys, I was thinking that it might be my last, that I might never see you again. We have so much catching up to do, my darling.'

'And all the time in the world to do it,' she said softly,

then back in doctor mode asked, 'What about the poor girl, Nathan? Is she injured or too cold to walk?'

'She'd fallen up there, hurt her leg badly, almost certainly has a fracture, so couldn't walk back down the fell side. She's also suffering from hypothermia due to not being able to move around in the cold, and needs her body heat brought back up in front of the fire, but not too near as it has to be a gradual thing to prevent shock.'

'And the young guy, what about him? He looks dreadful.'

'Yes, I know. He is totally traumatised by what has happened, thought they were going to die as their mobiles couldn't get a signal up there—it's totally impossible to do so. I'm going to give him something to calm him down. My bag is on the back seat of the car and I've got a relaxant in it that should do the trick. The guys from Mountain Rescue have phoned for an ambulance and as the weather has improved it should soon be here.'

She had been examining the girl's leg with gentle fingers and when he said, 'So was I right?'

She nodded. 'Yes, I would say a fracture of the tibia.'

He'd given the other teenager the relaxant and the youth was in a less traumatised state by the time the ambulance came. As it was about to set off with the two of them on board the boy's father phoned, having only just heard about the day's happenings, and promised that both he and his mother would be waiting for them in A and E when they got there, which helped to complete the calming-down process.

By the time that Nathan had changed back into his

suit and the three men and Libby had eaten the cooked breakfast that the hotel had provided, the night was almost gone. Soon it would be time to return to their homes, back to reality, work, school, and who knew what lay ahead of them now?

When they arrived back at her cottage he said jubilantly, 'Alone at last! I have things to say to you, Libby, that should have been said long ago. Come and sit beside me while I tell you all that is in my heart.

'I asked you to marry me once for the wrong reasons, didn't I?' he said soberly when she'd done as he asked. 'I was totally distraught knowing that Toby had been poisoned by the belladonna plant, and also because you were there like a rock to hold onto.

'I'm going to ask you again to be my wife, but there are things you need to know before I do that. When you told me that you loved me that day at the airport I realised that for the first time I was seeing you how you really were, beautiful, desirable and uncomplicated, but the timing was all wrong.

'When I kissed you goodbye after having told you in supreme arrogance that I wasn't interested in you, and that you should forget me, I knew that I wanted to stay and carry on from there with you. That I'd been blinkered, hadn't seen what was in front of me, since the kid who was forever at my heels when I was young had grown into the woman standing before me in tears.

'But I was so taken aback by the sudden revelation that I let you walk away and went to catch my flight, which was already being called, intending to get in touch the moment I arrived at my destination.

'When I got there I arrived to such a state of chaos at the hospital where I was going to work that I found that private lives were non-existent out there. We were on the job sometimes for twenty-four hours non-stop and even though I hadn't forgotten you I let the weeks and months go by. Dad used to phone me from time to time while I was out there and on one occasion he mentioned that you were marrying Jefferson on the coming Saturday. I knew then that I had to get to you before you married him and there was very little time to do so.

'I needed to ask you if you'd stopped loving me after the airport episode and had decided that he was the man you wanted. If you'd been able to tell me that he was, I would have left you in peace and lived with my own stupidity for the rest of my life.

'But my flight was delayed. I arrived at the church while the wedding ceremony was taking place. As I entered the porch the vicar had just pronounced you man and wife and you were smiling up at Jefferson like any happy bride would, so I had my answer, or thought I had.

'I couldn't get out of the church quickly enough and jumped onto a passing bus to get as far away as possible, then caught the next flight back to where I'd come from. So you see, Libby, I did come back for you, but not soon enough, and I've lived with the misery of knowing that ever since.'

She was listening to him aghast, with tears streaming down her face, unable to believe what he was saying, yet she knew Nathan wouldn't lie, he had no reason to. And he hadn't finished.

'I don't know if you will understand what I'm saying now,' he went on, 'but it was because of that and the hurt I did you that day when you came to see me off at the airport that I stayed away for so long.

'When I came back to Swallowbrook with Toby you had become just someone from my past, and since I've really got to know you I've found myself holding back all the time in case I hurt you again. Even after that fantastic night on the island I couldn't let *my* feelings, *my* needs ruin your life again.

'When you described what your life with Jefferson had been like I could have wept. But it was the smile you had for him that day in the church that threw me, which made me think you had married him for love.

'So now that you know how much I love and adore you, Libby, can we wipe the slate clean and start afresh with a wedding of our own, a life of our own, with Toby and our own children when they come along?'

'I married Ian on the rebound,' she said in a low voice, 'because you had made me feel so unloved, and the smile you saw was to convince those who I knew *did* care about me, such as both our fathers and other friends of long standing, that I wasn't making a big mistake, which of course I was.

'Yes, I will marry you, my dear love. To belong to you for always is all I've ever wanted. It will be all my dreams coming true, and with regard to giving Toby brothers and sisters I haven't checked it out properly yet, but mother nature is telling me that we might have taken care of that already on that wonderful night at Greystone House.'

'You mean that you might be pregnant? Oh, Libby, that would be fantastic!'

'It only occurred to me as I was getting ready this evening that I'd skipped a period for the first time ever, and I consoled myself with the thought that if you never did want me, at least I might be going to have some part of you in a child that we'd conceived.'

'Want you! I've never wanted anything more than you in my arms, in my bed, in my life for ever, so how about a Christmas wedding? But before that I have something to put on your finger.'

He produced a small velvet box from the inside pocket of his jacket and when he lifted the lid a beautiful emerald ring was revealed. As she gasped with delight he said, 'I chose it because the emerald is glowing and beautiful like the woman I love, but we can change it to a diamond if you wish.'

'How can you think that I would want to change something that you have chosen especially for me?' she asked breathlessly, and he took her hand in his and slipped it onto her finger.

As she looked down at it she said, 'I would love a Christmas wedding in Swallowbrook, Nathan, to be married in the village church with the bells ringing out across the snow that hopefully will have fallen to complete the day.'

He took her in his arms again and it felt like coming home after a long journey. Tears glistened on her lashes as the wonder of the moment took hold of her, and this time they were tears of happiness.

'You said that you also had something else to tell

me,' she reminded him in the last few moments before they had to separate while Nathan went to collect Toby from his father's house.

'It's just an idea that has been in my mind ever since I saw the house on the island, and I've followed it up by asking if it is available to rent for the Christmas period, and it is. So how would you like us to have our wedding reception there? Many of our guests will have their own boats and we could hire something bigger to transport those who haven't across the lake?'

'That would be magical,' she cried. 'Shall I ask the vicar if he can call round this evening to talk about the arrangements? He was saying only yesterday that he was disappointed that no one was planning a Christmas wedding, so he will be pleased to hear our news.'

The ring on her finger did not escape the notice of the surgery staff when she got into work later that morning and congratulations came from all sides. Nathan had told his father their good news when he'd gone to pick Toby up, and John called at the surgery during the morning to express his delight to his prospective daughter-in-law.

'You'd better tell your father to bring his best suit with him if he's going to be giving his daughter away,' he said laughingly, and remembering her father's pleasure when she'd rung him earlier with her news she thought that for once he was happy. Happier than he'd ever been since they'd lost her mother.

* * *

The vicar came round that evening as requested, and was, of course, delighted to hear that he was going to have a Christmas wedding in his church after all, and by the time he was ready to go the foundations of a wedding ceremony to take place on the morning of Christmas Eve had been laid.

'The main formality is that the banns, which are in the form of giving notice to anyone and everyone that a wedding has been arranged, must be read three times on three separate Sundays in a church before it can take place,' he told them. 'The rest of the procedure you will already know, I'm sure.

'December the twenty-fourth will be a special day for the folks of Swallowbrook this year,' he said as he was leaving. 'Two of its own marrying on that day, and both of them doctors from the health centre that is one of the main focal points of the village.'

Toby was fast asleep upstairs and when the vicar had gone they went up and stood by his bed. As they looked down at him Libby said, 'I wasn't wrong about us being in the baby business, Nathan. I've done a test and I'm pregnant.'

'Life is getting more wonderful by the minute,' he said chokingly. 'It wasn't so long ago that I wasn't sure if I would ever have children of my own because they would have had to have you as their mother and at the time the chances of that weren't looking good.'

'I was having the very same thoughts,' she told him, 'that if ever I had any children they would have to be yours.'

They sat talking long into the night, making plans,

dreaming dreams, and amongst them was the idea of making the two cottages into one.

The invitations had been sent, the details of the music they wanted given to the vicar, and the banns were being read. Libby's father would give her away. Hugo was to be Nathan's best man and Toby a pageboy.

Libby's best friend Melissa was cast in the role of matron of honour, and Keeley, a friend she'd always kept in touch with since they'd been at medical school, was to be a bridesmaid.

The ceremony would take place late morning and when it was over Libby and Nathan would sail cross the lake in *Pudding* to the house on the island where the reception was to take place in the afternoon. Outside caterers had been hired to prepare a buffet that would go on until everyone who wanted to come had been.

When they had all gone Toby would be tucked up in bed early to be ready for what Santa had brought while he'd been asleep. The problem of how he would get his sledge across the water had been on his mind at first, but they'd told him that he would bring it down from the sky on to the island and it would give the reindeer a chance to have a nibble at any grass that was lying around.

The day had dawned and though the sky was heavy and grey there was no snow, but Libby told herself it was expecting too much that the weather would adjust itself to her special requirements. She already had blessings by the score.

She was marrying the only man she'd ever loved in the church, in the village, where she'd lived all her life. She was carrying his child and was going to fill the gap, God willing, in the life of the small boy who was so dear to her heart.

That morning Nathan had told her that he was the interested party who had been quick to agree to a price when Greystone House had come onto the market, and that soon it would be theirs for holidays and weekends, and as she'd held him close she'd thought, what more could she want?

The church was full, the organist was playing the wedding march, and the bells were pealing out high above as Libby stood holding her father's arm on the same spot in the porch where Nathan had seen his hopes scattered all that time ago.

Today none of what had gone before mattered, they were together at last, and with a smile over her shoulder for her small pageboy and the two friends who had both travelled quite some distance to be with her on her special day, she lifted the hem of a wedding gown of heavy white brocade and, holding a bouquet of red Christmas roses, met her father's enquiring gaze and whispered, 'I'm ready, let's go.'

With every step she took towards Nathan, standing straight and still before the altar with Hugo by his side, the rightness of the moment increased. As he placed the gold band of matrimony on her finger next to the glowing emerald, the future was stretching before them as a wonderful dream that had become reality.

* * *

She was back in the church porch, holding onto the arm of her new husband this time, and as they stepped out into the open to be photographed they began to fall, soft and white, whirling and twirling—snowflakes from the sky above.

They were coming across the water, boats of all shapes and sizes, amongst them a big launch with lots of seating, and as Libby and Nathan waited to greet their guests on the landing stage of the island, with Toby holding both their hands, the lanterns around the lake came on early as a token of congratulation to the newlyweds.

'That will be one of my patients who works for the lake authorities making a gesture,' she said. 'People are so kind. If any of their craft go past we must signal for them to stop and invite them in for a bite, don't you think?'

'I *think* that you are wonderful,' he said laughingly. 'The whole world can stop by as far as I'm concerned as long as you are here with me to greet them.'

It was over. Their guests had gone back across the water with the moon to light their way home as well as the coloured lanterns.

Toby was asleep, having supervised leaving out wine and a mince pie for Santa Claus. Libby and Nathan had the night to themselves and as he removed the soft white cashmere stole from her shoulders, which she'd worn to keep out the cold, and unzipped her out of the long white dress, he held out his arms and after that it was

just the two of them, loving and giving each other all
the joys they had longed for and had sometimes thought
would never be theirs.

* * * * *

A sneaky peek at next month...

Medical Romance

CAPTIVATING MEDICAL DRAMA—WITH HEART

My wish list for next month's titles...

In stores from 2nd December 2011:

☐ New Doc in Town & Orphan Under the Christmas Tree
   — Meredith Webber

☐ The Night Before Christmas — Alison Roberts

& Once a Good Girl... — Wendy S. Marcus

☐ Surgeon in a Wedding Dress — Sue MacKay

☐ The Boy Who Made Them Love Again — Scarlet Wilson

Available at WHSmith, Tesco, Asda, Eason, Amazon and Apple

Just can't wait?

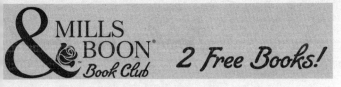

Have Your Say

You've just finished your book.
So what did you think?

We'd love to hear your thoughts on our
'Have your say' online panel
www.millsandboon.co.uk/haveyoursay

- 🌹 Easy to use
- 🌹 Short questionnaire
- 🌹 Chance to win Mills & Boon® goodies